THICKER THAN WATER

A Story of Hashknife Hartley

W. C. TUTTLE

SAGEBRUSH
Large Print Westerns

First published in Great Britain by Collins
First published in the United States by Houghton Mifflin

Published in Large Print 2011 by ISIS Publishing Ltd.,
7 Centremead, Osney Mead, Oxford OX2 0ES
by arrangement with
Golden West Literary Agency

The moral right of the author has been asserted

British Library Cataloguing in Publication Data
Tuttle, W. C. (Wilbur C.), 1883–1969.
   Thicker than water.
   1. Western stories.
   2. Large type books.
   I. Title
   813.5'4–dc22

ISBN 978–0–7531–8752–4 (pb)

Printed and bound in Great Britain by
T. J. International Ltd., Padstow, Cornwall

Contents

CHAPTER
ONE

The Ace of Spades

The two men faced each other across the little table in the living-room of the Circle Spade ranch-house, in the light of a single oil lamp. The younger of the two men was Jack McCoy, known as "Angel," while the other was Rance McCoy, his father, and owner of the Circle Spade ranch.

Angel McCoy was rather tall, well muscled, with features as clean-cut as a cameo. His skin was almost as white as milk, his hair as black as jet, and he wore it long in front of his ears — a swinging curl of inky-black against his white cheek. His eyes were brown, shaded by sharp-cut brows. There was no denying the fact that he was handsome.

Just now he wore a white silk shirt, with a red handkerchief knotted around his throat, black trousers tucked into the tops of a pair of fancy, high-heeled boots — and about him was an odor of perfume.

Rance McCoy's appearance had nothing in common with his son's. He was about fifty years of age, grizzled, hard-faced, with a skin the color of jerked venison. His eyes were gray, and there were scars on his face, which showed lighter than the rest of his skin; scars of many battles. Rance McCoy had been a fighter in his time. There were other scars, which did not show, where hot lead had scored him time and again.

He was tough, was Rance McCoy; an old gunman, afraid of nothing — not even of his handsome son.

"Well, all I can say is that you've got some damned queer ideas," said Angel slowly.

"Mebby I have," said the old man.

"No maybe about it," said Angel sneeringly. "Lila is of age and I'm of age. If I want to marry her, it's none of yore business."

"You think not? Well, everybody is entitled to an opinion. I've told yuh about me, Angel."

"Yeah, and I don't think much of yuh."

Angel got to his feet and stood there, looking down at his father.

"I knew all along that Lila wasn't my sister," he said slowly.

The old man lifted a hand to fend the light from his eyes, as he looked up at his son.

"Billy DuMond told yuh, Angel?"

"Ten years ago. He said you killed her father and then adopted her."

"That drunken thief!" muttered the old man.

"Who — Lila's father?"

"No — Billy DuMond."

"I don't know anythin' about that part of it," said Angel. "He merely told me that she wasn't my sister. You don't deny that, do yuh?"

"No, I don't deny it."

2

Angel slowly rolled a cigarette, watching the old man's face.

"Maybe you think I'm not good enough for her, eh? Was that why you were willin' to give me my share of the cattle, and let me buy out the Eagle? Wanted to get rid of me, eh?"

Angel laughed harshly and lighted his cigarette over the top of the lamp-chimney.

"There wasn't any question of gettin' rid of yuh," said Rance McCoy slowly. "It was yore own proposition. You wanted to run a saloon and be a gambler; so I gave yuh yore share of the cattle. I sent Lila away to school. It cost me a lot of money to educate her, Angel."

"I don't doubt that."

Angel exhaled a cloud of smoke through his shapely nostrils.

"But as far as you marryin' Lila — you'll not," declared Rance McCoy flatly. "I raised the two of yuh together, and I know all about both of yuh. I've heard that you're a crooked dealer, Angel. Men don't hint things like that unless there's some truth in it. Crooked at cards, crooked at everythin'."

Angel McCoy jerked forward, his dark eyes glittering in the yellow light.

"Crooked, am I?" he laughed harshly. "No man dares say it to my face. They come and whine to you, do they? And you believe things like this of yore own son! That's why you won't let me marry Lila, eh? All right; I'll tell Lila that she ain't yore daughter. I'll tell her you killed her father. I'll tell —"

3

"If yuh do" — Rance McCoy's old face twisted harshly and he leaned forward, shoving his right shoulder against the table — "If yuh do, Angel — I'll kill yuh. A long time ago yuh ceased to be my son. Oh, yuh'll get an even break. I never killed any man without givin' him an even break."

"Even break!" exclaimed Angel. "What man ever had an even break with you? I've seen yuh draw and shoot, old man."

The old man laughed mirthlessly. Few men could draw and shoot with Rance McCoy.

"Yuh always did lose yore nerve in a showdown," he said.

"I never lost my nerve," growled Angel. "But this ain't a shootin' proposition."

The old man studied him for a space of several minutes.

"Angel," he said slowly, "what does Lila know about this? She wouldn't marry her own brother. What have yuh told her?"

Angel smiled crookedly and rested his elbows on the table.

"Well, if you've got to know — she knows."

"She knows?"

"I told her tonight."

"Yuh told her tonight?"

"That you ain't her father — yes. No, I never asked her to marry me — not yet. But by God, I'm goin' to ask her!"

The old man got slowly to his feet, disclosing the fact that he wore a holstered gun. Angel also wore one, and the mother-of-pearl handle flashed like an opal in the yellow light. With a twitch of his left hand the old man jerked out a drawer from the table and produced an old deck of playing-cards.

He dropped them on the table and looked sharply at Angel, who was watching him curiously.

"Shuffle 'em," ordered the old man.

"What's the idea?"

"I'm givin' yuh an even break, Angel. You're a gambler, and I'm givin' yuh a gambler's chance. Shuffle the cards and let me cut 'em. You can do the dealin'. The one who gets the ace of spades — shoots first."

"You mean —" Angel hesitated.

"You know what I mean, yuh yaller pup."

Angel flushed quickly and reached for the cards. His long fingers riffled the cards with mechanical precision. Time after time he split the deck, until it seemed as though he was trying to wear out the cards. The old man's keen eyes watched those hands, and there was a half-smile on his lips.

"That's enough," he said drawlingly. "Let me cut."

It seemed to Angel that the old man studied the deck rather carefully before he made the cut.

"The one who gets the ace of spades shoots first, eh?" said Angel, and it seemed as though his voice trembled.

The old man nodded.

"Go ahead and deal."

Angel hesitated.

"This is foolishness, old man. If I shoot yuh, they'll hang me for murder. Lila's upstairs."

"She don't know you're here."

"But the shot would wake her up."

"How long do yuh think it'll take yuh to get away? You talk as though yuh already had the ace of spades. I'll take my chances. Go ahead and deal."

Angel shuddered slightly. It was all so ridiculous, this idea of dealing for the first shot. But the old man did not seem to mind. There was not a tremor in the gnarled hand that rested on the old table-top.

"Go ahead and deal, you coward," he said coldly.

With a flick of his fingers the gambler threw the first two cards — ace of hearts, six of clubs. There were fifty more cards in the deck.

King, jack. It was the king of spades.

"Hittin' close," said the old man.

Angel licked his lips and dealt the next two slowly — ten, deuce.

"How far for the first shot?" he asked hoarsely.

"Width of the room. Can't miss. Deal."

Queen, deuce.

"Runnin' small on yore side," observed the old man.

Angel licked his lips again and his right hand trembled, as he dealt himself a trey to Rance's second king.

"Why don'tcha git it over with, Angel?" taunted the old man. "Losin' yore nerve?"

But Angel did not reply. His eyes were staring at the cards as they fell. The deck was getting thin now. Not over a dozen cards left. It was difficult for him to swallow. The oil was low in the lamp, and it had begun to smoke a little.

Six cards left. Ace of diamonds, seven of hearts. Only four left. His hands felt heavy as lead. He wanted to say something, but his mouth was too dry. With a super-effort he managed to deal the next two cards — two deuces.

There were only two cards left in his hand; two old dog-eared cards that held his fate. He stared down at them as though fascinated. He looked across the table at the face of his father, who was laughing at him. Slowly his right hand went to his lips — a hand that trembled a tattoo against his mouth — and with a strangled word he dropped the two cards on the floor, turned on his heel, and stumbled to the door. He flung the door open, and a moment later came the staccato drumming of his horse's hoofs, as he rode swiftly away from the ranch.

The old man still stood beside the table, a half-smile on his lips, as he looked down at the cards. Then he stepped around the table and picked up those last two cards — a six of hearts and the joker. Then he swept up all the cards and opened the table drawer. Looking up at him from the bottom of the drawer was the ace of spades. It had been left there when the deck had been taken out.

"Busted his nerve," whispered the old man. "Lucky thing that old joker was bent enough to lift up the deck and give me a chance to cut it on the bottom. Still, I didn't think he had nerve enough to deal fifty of 'em — I wouldn't have had, that's a cinch."

CHAPTER
TWO

The Eagle Saloon

Angel McCoy rode back to Red Arrow, his mind filled with mixed emotions. Although it hurt him deeply, he was obliged to admit to himself that his father had out-gamed him. He tried to explain to his conscience that the whole thing had been a colossal piece of melodrama, and that he feared to get the ace of spades. He was a good shot. There was little doubt in his mind that his first shot would settle the whole argument, and he would be branded as a murderer.

There had never been any love lost between himself and his father. Their natures had always clashed. But Angel, even with his cold-blooded nature, did not want to be branded a parricide. The whole thing seemed so ridiculous now. Lila had been away to school for five years, and had returned a beautiful young lady, fit to turn the head of any man in the country. She was not his sister, and he could conceive of no reason why he should not marry her — if she was willing. She knew now that Rance McCoy was not her father, and, being of age, could do as she pleased.

Angel rode up to his own stable, at the rear of the Eagle saloon and gambling-house, put up his horse and entered the saloon by a rear door. The Eagle was rather a large place for a Western town, being an oblong room about sixty feet long by thirty feet wide. On the right-hand side was a long bar, while part of the center, with all the left-hand side, was taken up by tables and gambling paraphernalia.

At the rear of the saloon were two private rooms, one of which was used as sleeping-quarters by Angel. During the week there was little play at the Eagle, but on Saturday and Sunday, when the Red Arrow cowboys came to town, there was plenty of business.

The first man Angel McCoy met as he came into the place was Billy DuMond, a man as old as Rance McCoy, slouchy, unshaven, partly drunk. He was employed as a cowboy with the Half-Box R outfit, owned by "Butch" Reimer. Angel had known DuMond for years.

"Hyah, Angel," greeted DuMond owlishly.

"Hello, Billy. I was kinda hopin' I'd see yuh."

Angel drew DuMond aside and lowered his voice.

"I just had a run-in with the old man, Billy. He knows you told me about Lila; so yuh better steer clear of him."

DuMond wiped his mouth with the back of his hand and swallowed dryly.

"Lemme git yuh straight, Angel. Yuh told him I said it?"

"Yeah; that he killed Lila's father and then adopted her. You told me about it ten years ago, yuh remember."

9

"Uh-huh. Well" — DuMond cuffed his shapeless hat over one ear and stared at Angel — "Well, what did yuh drag me into it fer? I don't want no trouble."

"A man don't get into trouble by tellin' the truth."

"Th' hell they don't! I knowed a horse-thief that told the truth — and they hung him. And you told old Rance McCoy that I said — I — Angel, I'm shore sorry yuh told it."

"You scared of him, Billy?"

"Well, by God!" snorted DuMond, cuffing his hat to the opposite side of his head. "Any old time I git m' spark of life blowed out, who's goin' to light her ag'in? Don't you re'lize that yore old man is danger's? He'll shoot."

Angel laughed shortly.

"I reckon you're right, Billy; I'm sorry."

"Sorrow won't help me none."

"Did yuh know Lila's father?"

"No! I don't know nothin'! I don't even 'member tellin' yuh anythin'. Ten years ago! Must 'a' been drunk. Who's this here Lila you're talkin' about, Angel?"

"Oh, go to hell!" snorted Angel, and went on toward the bar, where he met Butch Reimer and Dell Blackwell, one of Reimer's cowboys. Butch Reimer was of medium height, with wide shoulders and a face that might well have belonged to a prize-fighter of the old bare-knuckle school. Several years previous to this time Butch had been kicked square in the face by a sharp-shod horse. There were no plastic surgeons at that time, so Butch's face had merely healed up, leaving a crooked nose, twisted mouth, and a misplaced eyebrow, not to mention numerous indentations never intended by Nature in her most uncritical moods.

Dell Blackwell was a lithe, olive-complexioned, black-haired cowboy; inveterate gambler, bronco rider, and reputed a bad man to start trouble with.

"I just got nicked for a hundred in yore ecarte game," growled Butch. "Drew a four and a five; but the dealer turned a natural."

"Butch had a system," smiled Blackwell. "Always won his first bet, yuh know; so he slapped down a hundred as a first bet. What's new, Angel?"

"Not a damned thing, Dell."

"Have a drink," growled Butch. "I hear Lila's home."

"Yeah," said Angel shortly.

"Growed up much?"

"Sure."

"You're sure talkative. Where yuh been — out to see the old man?"

Angel nodded moodily.

"I thought so," grinned Butch, as he filled his glass. He knew that Angel and his father usually quarreled.

"What made yuh think that?" demanded Angel.

"Jist from yore actions. Oh, I don't blame yuh. He jist the same as told me to keep off his place last week. And I'm goin' to stay off, too. Ask Dell why."

"Cinch," laughed Dell. "I dropped in there a couple weeks ago and found the old man practicin'. I tell yuh, he was shootin' pepper cans off the corral fence at sixty feet. Stuck up six in a row, about two feet apart, and hit every danged one of 'em. You jist try hittin' three-inch squares every time at sixty feet with a forty-five."

"I can jist hit my hat at that distance," grinned Butch, "and I wear the widest thing Stetson makes."

"And you jist shoot good enough to win my money," laughed Blackwell.

"Somebody will kill him one of these days," said Angel.

"Yeah — send him a bomb by express. Let's have another."

CHAPTER
THREE

Lila's Departure

Morning at the Circle Spade still found Rance McCoy humped in his chair beside the table in the old living-room. The lamp had burned dry long since, and the chimney was soot-streaked. "Chuckwalla Ike" Hazen, the old cook, was in the kitchen, wrestling with the cooking utensils. Chuckwalla Ike was as old as Rance McCoy, a weather-beaten old desert cook, crooked in the legs from riding bad horses in his youth, with his left elbow slightly out of line from stopping a bullet.

Chuckwalla wore a long, sad-looking mustache, and his head was as bald as a baseball. His nose was generous, and one cheek was habitually pouched from tobacco. He was clad in a sleeveless undershirt, overalls, and moccasins, as he peered into the living-room at Rance McCoy.

"Up kinda early ain't yuh, Rance?" he drawled. "I was — uh — I reckon I better put me on a shirt. Plumb forgot we've got a lady among us. Say, whatsa matter with yuh? Look like hell this mornin'."

"I'm all right," said Rance huskily.

"Which yuh ain't a-tall. Yuh can't fool Chuckwalla. What time does the Queen of Sheber come among us f'r nourishment?"

"I dunno," wearily.

"Well, I s'pose not."

Chuckwalla scratched his shoulder against a corner of the doorway.

"She shore growed up purty, didn't she, Rance? Five year ago she was a tow-headed kid with long legs and freckles, and she used to yell at me, 'Chuckwalla Ike, go set on a spike,' and now she pokes out her hand and says, 'Mr. Hazen, how do yuh do.' There's only one thing that improves with age, and that's liquor."

"They grow up," said Rance slowly.

"Don't they? Well, I s'pose I'd better scare up a flock of biscuits. She allus liked 'em. Mebby I better put on a shirt. She might not like a cook in dishabelle, as they say. And my lingeree is kinda mournful, too. And yuh might tell Monty Adams and Steve Winchell to cut out their profane greetin's to me this mornin'. As far as the human voice is concerned, this ranch-house leaks like a sieve."

Rance McCoy turned his head and looked curiously at old Chuckwalla.

"You heard what was said last night?"

"That don't bother me," said Chuckwalla quickly. "But I shore was curious to know who got that black ace, and quit on the job."

"I got it," said Rance softly, glancing toward the stairs.

14

"Uh-huh." Chuckwalla opened his mouth widely, blinked his eyes and backed toward the stove, where he turned and began shaking up the fire. Rance walked out to the front porch, and the old cook looked after him, a quizzical expression in his eyes.

"Rance," he said to himself, "you're addin' lies to the rest of yore sins."

Rance McCoy sat down on the steps of the old ranch-house which had been his home for eighteen years. There were a few stunted rosebushes in the yard. Near the corner of the house grew a gnarled cottonwood tree. The barbed-wire fence sagged badly in spots, and the weeds grew unmolested. To his left was the long, low stable, and beyond it was the series of pole-corrals. On the hill beyond the stable a bunch of cattle were stringing away from the ranch water-hole in the willows. Several miles away to the south he could see a streamer of black smoke from a train, heading toward Red Arrow, northwest of the ranch.

The Circle Spade had never been a big cattle outfit. Only two cowboys were employed by Rance McCoy. He had never been well liked in the Red Arrow country. Gun-men are usually respected, but rarely liked. They let old Rance alone when he came to town and got drunk, which he did at rare intervals; but never blind drunk.

He could hear Monty Adams and Steve Winchell, the two cowboys, noisily washing their faces at the old wash-bench near the kitchen door, and joking with Chuckwalla Ike. Came a step on the porch, and he turned to see Lila. She was a tall, slender girl, her

15

shapely head piled high with a wealth of golden-blonde hair, and wearing a pale blue dress.

Her eyes were slightly red, as though she had been crying. She leaned against the left side of the doorway and looked at the man she had always believed to be her father.

"How didja sleep, Lila?" he asked.

She shook her head slowly.

"Not very well."

"Uh-huh."

His shoulders hunched beneath his coarse blue shirt, and he turned his gaze away from her.

"Well, go ahead," he said slowly. "No use sparrin' around. Angel told yuh a lot of things last night, didn't he?"

"Yes."

"Well, what do yuh think about it?"

"Oh, I don't know what to think. He said you killed my father."

Old Rance lifted his head and stared across the hills, his left hand caressing his stubbled chin.

"Yeah, he told me the same thing, Lila."

"I heard what was said."

"Didja? What did yuh hear?"

"You — you forced him to deal those cards."

Rance laughed harshly.

"Busted his nerve, didn't I?"

"Did you? Do you suppose he would have shot you, if he had drawn the card?"

"I hope so; I hate a quitter."

"But you are his father!"

"It never meant much to Angel."

"Would you have shot him?"

"If I had drawn that ace of spades — sure."

She did not know that the ace of spades had been left in the drawer.

"Where is my father buried?" asked Lila softly.

Rance McCoy shook his head.

"I can't tell yuh, Lila."

"Does Billy DuMond know?"

"He don't know anythin' about it, except what he heard."

Chuckwalla Ike came to the doorway and called:

"You folks ready to eat?"

"Better go in and eat, Lila," said Rance.

But Lila shook her head, and after a sharp glance at Rance McCoy, Chuckwalla went back to the kitchen, complaining to himself.

"Where is my mother?" asked Lila.

"Yore mother?" Rance frowned heavily. "Oh, yeah — yore mother. Well, I dunno, Lila."

"Didn't my father tell you?"

"No-o-o, he didn't say."

"But you killed him."

Rance McCoy hunched his shoulders helplessly.

"Let's me and you not talk about it, Lila. It's all gone and forgotten now. You've been my little girl ever since yuh wasn't knee-high to a nail; you're still my little girl."

The old man's voice was not very steady and he did not look at her.

17

"It's not forgotten," said Lila bitterly. "Why didn't you tell me a long time ago? I haven't any right to — I'm not your daughter. You haven't any adoption papers, have you?"

Rance shook his head sadly.

"Wasn't anything like that, Lila. I didn't never want yuh to know. I wish I'd killed Billy DuMond before he ever told Angel. The drunken bum ain't hardly fit to hang on the hot end of a bullet. Angel wants to marry yuh, Lila. Mebby yuh heard him say it last night. But don't do it."

"That has nothing to do with the case," said Lila evenly. "You know I can't stay here any longer."

Old Rance turned and looked keenly at her.

"Yuh — uh — yuh can't stay here?" he faltered.

"Don't you see how it is?" she said helplessly. "I don't belong here. I — I'll try and pay you back for what I've cost you. I don't know how it can be done, but I'll try. You've been good to me."

Lila turned abruptly on her heel and went back into the house. The old man sank a little lower on the step, when he heard her tell Chuckwalla she did not want any breakfast. She was talking to the two cowboys, but Rance could not hear what was said.

A few minutes later Monty Adams came out to him. He was industriously picking his teeth and trying to appear at ease. Monty was tow-headed, rather flat-faced, and of medium height.

"Lila asked me to hitch up the buckboard and take her to town," said Monty. "Is it all right, Rance?"

"Sure."

Rance cleared his throat harshly, but did not look around. When Monty went back into the house Rance got up and walked down to the stable, where he sat down on an overturned box and looked gloomily at the ranch-house. He watched Monty and Steve hitch up the old buckboard, and saw Chuckwalla carry Lila's trunk out to the ranch-house porch.

There was no good-bye spoken. Lila came down and Steve helped her into the vehicle. She shook hands with Chuckwalla, and drove away with Monty. Steve sauntered down to the bunk-house, followed by a collie pup, which carried a piece of board in its mouth, while Chuckwalla sat down on the porch and rolled a cigarette.

He looked up quizzically as Rance came up to the porch, but the owner of the Circle Spade said nothing. For possibly five minutes they sat there together, saying nothing. Chuckwalla was the first to break the silence.

"Wimmin," he said solemnly, "do beat hell."

"Men, too," said Rance sadly.

"Yeah, that's right, Rance; they shore do. If I was you, I'd slap Billy DuMond to a peak and then kick the peak off."

Rance McCoy smiled bitterly.

"What would yuh gain by that, Chuckwalla?"

"I dunno. Mebby he ain't worth the effort, Rance. Oh, you can set there and pull yore old poker-face, Rance McCoy. But I know yuh. I know how yuh feel toward Lila. It's jist like takin' pincers and pullin' out yore finger-nails. I may not have a lot of brains, but I ain't dumb.

19

"She ain't showin' any sense, I tell yuh. My God, you've done everythin' for her. What if yuh ain't her daddy? Yuh shore been good to her, old-timer. Even if you did kill her real father. I don't know a thing about it, and I don't want to. I've been with you goin' onto eight year, Rance; and her own dad couldn't 'a' been better to her. It's that school she's been to. They done give her top-heavy ideas, that's what."

"I know," said Rance softly. "But don't blame her too much. It was a shock to her, Chuckwalla."

"To know you killed her dad? Shucks, what's that? She didn't know him no better than I knowed Gineral Custer — and I don't hold no grudge ag'in' the Injuns. That's why I allus say that wimmin do beat hell. There ain't never been no wimmin in my life, Rance. And I was a likely critter in m' youth. Lotsa girls looked sideways at me."

"And now you're jist a cow-outfit cook," said Rance seriously.

"Yea-a-ah — and what are you? Owner of the outfit; eatin' your tough old heart out over a girl that don't deserve it; father of a son that ort to be kicked in the pants and showed the error of his ways. You ain't got no edge on me, Rance. I tell yuh what I would like to do. How much money have I got comin'?"

"About eighty dollars, Chuckwalla."

"Plenty. I've got a notion to go to Red Arrer and git so drunk that all m' previous libations would look like the mornin' meal of a day-old calf. I ain't been drunk since they quit callin' the Platte River Nee-brath-kah. That's what's makin' us old, Rance. By God, pretty

20

soon me and you will be so old we'll be preachin' temp'-rance."

Old Rance shook his head sadly.

"I'd be scared to, Chuckwalla. If I got six drinks under my hide, I'd kill somebody."

"Well, don't be so finicky about it. Come on in and throw some ham and aigs into yuh. Yessir, I b'lieve it's time that me and you blowed off steam. Eighty dollars, eh? Sounds like joy-bells to me. Jist forget that little lady with the queer ideas. If she marries that jug-headed son of yours, she'll still be in the fambly."

Monty Adams took Lila to Red Arrow and she got a room at the Valley Hotel. She had little to say to Monty on the way to town, except that she would probably stay in Red Arrow until she heard from some friends in the East. Angel saw them drive up to the hotel, and lost no time in joining them. When he saw Lila's baggage he knew she had left the Circle Spade, and was secretly glad. Monty drove the team over to the Eagle Saloon, leaving Lila and Angel together.

"I left the ranch," she said simply.

"That's what I thought, Lila. Well, I suppose it was the best thing to do. What are yore plans?"

"I haven't any, Angel. I just think in circles. But first of all I want to have a talk with Billy DuMond."

"I'm afraid yuh won't," smiled Angel. "Bill is scared of his life. I told him the old man knew what he told me. He's scared of Rance McCoy — and I don't blame him."

"Not after what happened last night," said Lila.

Angel's face flushed hotly.

"You heard that, Lila?"

"I did."

"I'm sorry about that. But it doesn't matter, I suppose. I lost my nerve, Lila. It was one of the most cold-blooded games I ever heard about. But that was like him. The man has no conscience, no nerves at all. He's a born killer. Friendship means nothin' to him."

"I wonder if it does," sighed Lila.

"Not a thing in the world. He don't know the meanin' of the word friendship. Oh, I don't care if he is my father. I'm old enough to know things. He's been good to me, in his own queer way. But we never agreed. Last night was the climax. If he had drawn that ace of spades, he'd have killed me."

"I think he would," said Lila. "Anyway, he said he would."

"And been glad of the chance," growled Angel. "Well, I'm all through with him. I'll get somebody to help put yore trunk into the hotel, Lila. You just stay here until yuh make up yore mind what yuh want to do, and don't worry about the money end of it. The owner of this hotel owes me a fat gamblin' bill, and this will be a good way to collect it."

CHAPTER
FOUR

Chuckwalla Makes a Mistake

In spite of the fact that the town of Red Arrow was on a transcontinental railroad, and with the advantages of being a county seat, it had never grown beyond its original cow-town stage. Perhaps it was because no one was interested in Red Arrow, except those who lived there before the railroad came through the valley. It was not a division point, and many of the trains only stopped on flag.

Red Arrow Valley was about ten miles wide at this point, with the Little Smoky range on the west and the old lava beds on the east. The valley ran southeast, and the Red Arrow River ambled its way down through the valley with many a twist and turn.

The nearest town to Red Arrow was Welcome, fifteen miles to the southeast. Between Red Arrow and Welcome was the Curlew Spur, where loading-pens had long been installed for the convenience of the cattlemen south of Red Arrow.

The Circle Spade ranch was about six miles slightly south of east from Red Arrow. Directly south, and about the same distance from town, was Butch Reimer's Half-Box R. Northeast, five miles from town, was the JML outfit, owned by Jim Langley, and about three miles north of town, on Coyote Creek, was the 77 horse outfit, owned by Henry Cave.

Red Arrow town had a business district which was really only about one long block in length by a short block in width. The buildings were all of weather-beaten frame structure, *sans* paint. The Valley Hotel and the court-house were two-story buildings, but the biggest structure was the livery stable. The streets were of three varieties — dust, snow, or mud, according to the season.

The long arm of the law was represented by Slim Caldwell, sheriff, and two deputies, "Chuck" Ring and "Scotty" McKay. Prior to becoming a citizen of Red Arrow and getting himself elected sheriff of the county, Caldwell had been a Texas Ranger. Scotty McKay almost became a member of the famous Royal Northwest Mounted Police. The only thing that kept him out was the fact that he wasn't able to qualify. Scotty was a bow-legged little Scot, with a tilted nose, a bushy head of sandy hair, and an exalted opinion of Scotty McKay.

Chuck Ring was a huge figure of a man, with a voice like a bull, a huge mop of black hair, and about as gentle as a playful grizzly. Chuck was prone to gross exaggerations. A single rattlesnake, according to Chuck, became a "million of the darned things." At times his imagination soared to such heights that he even astonished Caldwell, who was no second-rate liar himself.

It was nearing the middle of the afternoon when Rance McCoy and Chuckwalla Ike came to Red Arrow. They tied their horses at the Eagle hitch-rack and went across the street to the Cattlemen's Bank, where Rance McCoy drew enough money to cause the cashier considerable wonder.

"You're pullin' out quite a hunk, ain't cha?" queried Chuckwalla, rather amazed at Rance.

"Why not?" asked Rance gloomily. "It ain't worth nothin' to me — now."

Chuckwalla understood. Old Rance had saved for Lila. He had given Angel his share of the Circle Spade; so now there was no inducement left for him to make or save money. He gave Chuckwalla eighty dollars, and they went back to the street, where they stood on the edge of the wooden sidewalk and studied the situation.

"Whatcha want to do?" asked Rance.

"Git drunk," said Chuckwalla. "O-o-o-oh, there is a land of co-o-o-orn and wi-i-i-ine, and all its riches truly mi-i-i-ine."

"Don't sing."

"I forgot, Rance."

They stepped off the sidewalk and went diagonally across the street and up to the Red Arrow Saloon. Rance had never been in the Eagle Saloon since Angel had bought it.

Butch Reimer was standing at the bar, talking with the bartender when Rance and Chuckwalla came in.

25

Butch had been drinking quite heavily, and his tongue was noticeably thick.

"Hyah, Rance," he said, grinning broadly. "Well, if here ain't old Chuckwalla Ike! What'r yuh doin' — celebratin' a birthday?"

"Yuh might say we are," agreed Chuckwalla, yanking hard on one side of his mustache. "What'r yuh absorbin', Butch?"

"Cawn juice," drawled Butch. "Say, Rance, I heard yuh was lookin' for Billy DuMond."

Old Rance shot him a sidelong glance.

"Didja?"

"Yeah."

They drank thirstily and clattered their glasses on the bar.

"Holy hell!" snorted Chuckwalla. "Either I'm gettin' awful neck-tender, or they're puttin' dynamite in the hooch. I jist laid m'self a blister from gullet to gut. Whooee-e-e!"

"That stuff is twenty year old," declared the bartender.

"Yeah, it's shore got all its teeth."

"You're gettin' old," declared Butch, laughing.

"Like hell, I am!" flared Chuckwalla. "When I left Gila Flats I was the best man in a radium of fifty miles, and I been gettin' better every day. I ain't never run, and I ain't never been whipped. Gimme more of that venom."

For more than an hour they leaned against the bar and drank what was commonly known as "rot-gut." Chuckwalla grew mellow, but it did not seem to affect old Rance. He became just a trifle more serious, more polite. Several times he hitched his holster to a more convenient position, and Butch blinked thoughtfully.

"You spoke about Billy DuMond," reminded old Rance.

"Yeah, I did," admitted Butch.

"He's still with yuh, ain't he?"

"Oh, sure."

"Yeah."

That was all. Old Rance took his drinks calmly. Chuckwalla sang bits of songs, using the same tune for all of them. Butch wondered if it wouldn't be a good idea for him to warn Billy DuMond to keep out of Red Arrow. But Butch was getting rather drunk, and his friendship with DuMond became of less consequence with each successive drink.

Finally old Rance sighed deeply and announced his intentions of going to the Eagle Saloon.

"Tha's a good idea," agreed Chuckwalla. "Le's have a little action. C'mon."

They went down the street to the Eagle, and went inside. Angel was in a poker game, and he looked curiously at his father and his two undeniably drunk companions. He felt that his father had absorbed just as much liquor as the other two.

They had a drink. Old Rance hooked his elbows over the top of the bar and gazed around his son's premises. It was the first time he had ever been in there since Angel had owned it. Angel, apparently absorbed in his game, kept an eye on the old man, who walked steadily over to a black-jack table, where one cowboy was

27

making two-bit bets, and threw down a twenty-dollar bill.

His two cards showed an ace and a jack — a natural — and the dealer paid him thirty dollars. Old Rance left the fifty on the board. He won on the next deal, and let the hundred ride. The dealer looked curiously at the hard-faced old man. Hundred-dollar bets were uncommon at black-jack.

Another ace and a jack fell to the old man, and the dealer counted out a hundred and fifty. That was left with the hundred, and again the old man won. There was now five hundred in front of old Rance.

"You playin' for the pile?" queried the dealer.

Old Rance nodded. His two cards showed two kings. After a moment of inspection he drew out his roll of bills, counted out another five hundred, split the two kings, and indicated that he would make a double bet. His next two cards were an ace and a queen, making him twenty-one and twenty. The best the dealer could do was to make eighteen.

Slowly he counted out the money to old Rance — one thousand dollars. There was now two thousand on the board. The dealer wet his lips and stared at the old man. He shifted his gaze and looked at Angel, who got up from the poker game and came over to the black-jack layout.

"Deal," said the old man. The dealer looked at Angel for some kind of a signal.

"Two-thousand-dollar bet," said the dealer nervously.

"Hundred dollars is the limit," said Angel softly.

Old Rance looked coldly upon his son.

"I thought yuh run a gamblin'-house," he said. "Yuh can play for a hundred in the bunk-houses."

"I've got sixty dollars in the bank," said the dealer.

"Take yore money and go home," said Angel.

"No nerve, eh?"

"I don't want yore money."

"You're a liar — you're jist scared."

Angel flushed hotly and shoved the dealer aside, picking up the deck, facing the cards, and began shuffling them. The poker-players halted their game and came over to the layout.

"Two thousand dollars that you get the ace of spades," said old Rance softly.

Angel did not look up from the cards, as he said:

"This is black-jack; place yore bets."

"Two thousand," said old Rance.

Angel dealt snappily, and old Rance's hand showed a six and a deuce. Quickly he covered the cards, indicating that he would not draw. Angel turned over a king and a five. He studied them thoughtfully. He did not think there was a chance in a thousand that his father would stand pat on less than seventeen. Then he drew his card — a seven-spot — making him twenty-two.

With a flip of his fingers he turned over the old man's cards — six and a deuce; a total of eight. For several moments he stared at his father. If he had stood on his original fifteen, he would have won the money.

"Mebby I'll git a natural next deal," said the old man. "Gimme my two thousand, and deal for the pile."

"Four thousand?" whispered Angel haltingly.

29

"Shore. A natural would win me six thousand."

Angel hesitated. Four thousand dollars was more than the Eagle could afford to lose. Still, he might win. It was against the law of averages for the old man to continue winning. He had won six times straight already.

"Deal 'em," growled the old man.

Slowly Angel dealt the four cards. Old Rance turned his two cards face-up on the table — a ten and a five.

"Hit 'em," he said.

Angel flipped the card to the table. It was a six, making old Rance's count twenty-one. Angel turned over his cards, disclosing a jack and a seven, making a count of seventeen. If old Rance had not disclosed his hand, Angel would not have drawn. But now he was obliged to draw. His first card was a deuce. Angel swallowed heavily and flipped the next card. It was an ace. His hand counted twenty. Another ace would give him a tie with the old man.

With an exaggerated motion of his two hands holding the deck, he quickly stripped off a card and flipped it over. It was the ace of spades. Not a word was spoken for several moments.

"The house takes half of all ties," said Angel coldly.

"You've got yore half," said old Rance dully. "You never put up yore two thousand. Deal 'em ag'in."

Angel shuffled them carefully, taking plenty of time, and when the old man cut the cards, no one seemed to know that Angel slipped the cut, and the cards were back where they were before the cut.

Old Rance drew a queen and a trey, while Angel's hand showed an ace and a jack — a natural. He swept in the two thousand, a grin of derision on his lips. For a long time the old man looked down at the green top of the table. He heaved a deep sigh and dug down in his pocket, drawing out the money he had received from the bank. It totaled nineteen hundred and eighty dollars — what was left of his twenty-five hundred. He spread the bills out on the table.

"Deal," he said softly.

"One bet?" asked Angel.

"Jist one."

"You ort to deal, Rance," said Chuckwalla.

Angel looked quickly at the old cook.

"Where do you come in on this?" he demanded.

"Jist the same, I think he ort to deal."

"Oh, all right."

Angel shoved the deck over to old Rance, who shuffled them carefully, and dealt himself a count of sixteen.

"You draw first," said Angel. "You're playin' against the house."

"I'm set. How many do yuh need."

"I pay eighteen," said Angel hoarsely, indicating that he had seventeen.

Old Rance shook his head sadly and turned away from the table. Angel smiled and looked for the deck of cards, as he picked up the money, but the deck had disappeared. The only cards on the table were the two two-card hands, with only old Rance's two face-up.

"Who took that deck?" demanded Angel quickly.

But no one seemed to know. Old Rance and Chuckwalla were already outside the place.

"That's damned funny!" snorted Angel hotly.

"You got damned well paid for it," laughed one of the men.

"Yeah?" Angel swept up the money and went to the rear of the room. The loss of that deck seemed to annoy him. He came back and walked to a front window, where he looked out. Old Rance had gone into the Shanghai Café, but Chuckwalla was sitting on the sidewalk, looking through what appeared to be a deck of cards.

Old Chuckwalla was drunkenly deliberate. He sorted out the different suits, holding them between his knees. Chuck Ring and Scotty McKay came along, and stopped to watch the old cook.

"Ar-re ye fixin' to tr-r-rim somebody?" asked Scotty.

"Betcher life," grunted Chuckwalla.

"You're drunk, Chuckwalla," boomed Chuck Ring. "Lemme fix up yore deck. I shore can mingle a cold-deck, if I've got plenty time."

"Let 'em alone," said Chuckwalla seriously. He put all the suits together, got unsteadily to his feet, and went into the café, where he found old Rance seated at a table. Chuckwalla sat down heavily at the opposite side of the table and leaned on his elbows.

"Rance," he said solemnly, "you're a fool."

Old Rance squinted painfully at Chuckwalla, but said nothing.

"'F I remember rightly, yuh never even seen the seventeen that Angel had in his last hand."

Rance shook his head slowly.

"Yuh had the king of clubs and the six of hearts, Rance. Look at this."

Chuckwalla took the deck from his pocket and spread out the club and heart suits. It showed a missing king and a six-spot. Rance lifted his eyes and looked inquiringly at Chuckwalla, who spread the other two suits. The ten of diamonds, trey of spades, and the ace of spades were missing.

"He had the ten of diamonds and the trey of spades in his last hand," said Chuckwalla angrily.

"What about that ace of spades?" asked old Rance.

"He held that out, you danged fool!" exploded Chuckwalla. "He stole that ace of spades to keep yuh from winnin' four thousand dollars from him, and he stole it ag'in, t' use in case he needed it."

Old Rance shifted his eyes thoughtfully.

"'F I was you, I'd go back and kill him, Rance," declared Chuckwalla. "Son or no son — he's a thief."

Old Rance turned his eyes back to Chuckwalla.

"He didn't steal that last pot, Chuckwalla. He miscounted his hand. I should have looked at it."

"He stole the ace of spades on yuh."

"Did yuh see him steal it?"

"No, but he did."

"Yuh can't prove it, Chuckwalla."

"I can't prove he did — no! But it ain't in the deck; so he must 'a' stole it ag'in."

"And that's yore only evidence that he played crooked?"

"What more do yuh want?"

Old Rance slowly reached in his pocket and took out the ace of spades.

"The ace of spades is a fav'rite card of mine," he said slowly. "And I don't like to have folks use it ag'in' me. What are yuh goin' to eat, Chuckwalla?"

The old cook lifted his eyes from the ace of spades and looked at the bland-faced Chinaman, who was waiting to take their order.

"Got any crow, Charley?"

"Clow?" The Chinaman blinked.

"Big, black bird, Charley."

"Oh, yessa; I sabe clow. Me no got. You like clow?"

"Sometimes I have t' eat it, Charley. Better bring me some ham and aigs."

CHAPTER
FIVE

Father and Son

In the meantime Chuck Ring and Scotty McKay had gone to the Eagle, where they learned that Angel had won twenty-five hundred dollars from old Rance McCoy.

"That's a lot of money," declared Chuck, accepting a drink on the house. "I seen old Chuckwalla separatin' the suits of a deck of cards over there on the sidewalk, and I wondered who he was tryin' to freeze a deck onto. Here's how, gents."

"Separatin' the suits, eh?" said Angel thoughtfully.

"I'll bet that was yore deck," said one of the men. "But what was his idea of separatin' the suits, I wonder?"

"Probably tryin' to see if it was a full deck," laughed the bartender.

"Well, he ought to know it wasn't. There was four cards left on the table. I saw Angel tear 'em up and throw 'em in a cuspidor. Old Chuckwalla Ike's drunk."

Angel nodded slowly, thoughtfully. He knew — and deep in his soul he cursed old Chuckwalla heartily, as he turned away from the bar and went back to his room.

"Kind of a funny deal," said one of the men. "It ain't none of my business, but nobody seen Angel's cards on that last deal. He jist said he'd pay eighteen, which would indicate that he had seventeen. But did he? The old man walked right out, and Angel tore up them four cards."

"He wouldn't cheat his own father, would he?" asked Chuck.

"I didn't say he did. But on one hand he drew a deuce, ace, ace, to tie the old man's twenty-one."

"That don't pr-r-rove anythin'," said Scotty.

"It don't. But if it had been anythin' but an ace, it would have busted the Eagle."

"The divil looks after his own — mebby," grinned Scotty.

"With a little personal assistance," laughed Chuck. "But it's nothin' to us. Personally, I like Angel. The old man is a hard character. But as far as that's concerned, none of us are growin' any wings."

Later on in the evening Billy DuMond came to town, and Angel took him to the hotel to see Lila. DuMond didn't want to go. He had been sure to find out that Rance McCoy was not in town before he would come in, and he didn't want to say anything more. But Angel insisted that he tell Lila all he knew about it.

They went up to Lila's room, and Billy DuMond slouched on the edge of a hard chair, doubling his old hat in his nervous hands.

"Like I told Angel — I dunno anythin'," he said to Lila. "I jist heard things a long time ago, and I — I prob'ly was drunk when I told Angel what I did."

"What did you tell Angel?" asked Lila.

DuMond twisted the hat a few more times.

"Well, I dunno how true it is. A feller told me a long time ago that you wasn't Rance McCoy's girl. He said yore name was Stevens, and that old Rance killed yore father in a gun-fight. You was a little baby, I reckon, and there wasn't no place to put yuh. Angel's mother jist died a while before that, and somehow old Rance kinda adopted yuh."

"And that is all you know about it?"

"Yes'm. I don't want to git dragged into it, ma'am. It's none of my business."

"And my father's name was Stevens?"

"That's the name."

"And where did all this happen?"

"I ain't right sure," said DuMond. "It seems to me that it was in the Twisted River country. This feller that told me about it mentioned a town named Medicine Tree. It's been a long time ago, yuh know; and I might be mistaken."

"Thank you very much," said Lila.

"Oh, you're welcome, ma'am."

DuMond got to his feet, thankful that the interview was over.

"I — I hope yuh won't say nothin' to Rance McCoy."

"Don't mind him," said Angel quickly.

"That's all right t' say," DuMond grinned sourly.

After Billy DuMond had left the room, Angel asked Lila what she intended doing.

"You heard what I told the old man the other night, Lila. When I said I wanted to marry you, I told the truth."

"But I don't want to marry anybody — yet," said Lila. "My mind is all upset and I hardly know what to do. Angel, I was wondering if they have already engaged the teacher for the coming term of school? I could qualify, I think."

"We can find out, Lila. I know the trustees. But I'd a lot rather have yuh marry me. I'm makin' good money."

"Not yet, Angel."

"Well, all right," grudgingly. "I'll find out about the school. But you know what I told the old man, Lila. You're goin' to marry me some day. How are yuh fixed for money?"

"I have enough — if I get that school."

"Well, if yuh need any — just yelp."

Lila promised she would, and Angel went back to his business.

But in spite of the fact that Angel was well liked by the cattlemen of the Red Arrow country, his trade fell off badly in the following days. Where he had been able to use four dealers, he was now able to handle his games with but two men. On the next payday the Red Arrow Saloon got the big play.

Nothing was said, but Angel knew that in winning the twenty-five hundred from his father he had caused somebody to have a deep, dark suspicion that there had been something crooked about the game. And this suspicion had been voiced sufficiently to cause the gambling public to seek their games elsewhere.

Angel had made no effort to see the school trustees in behalf of Lila. He did not want her to teach the school. That savored too much of independence — and Angel did not want Lila to be independent. He did not know that she had seen them and had secured the position, because she did not mention it until everything was settled.

Old Rance McCoy received the news with a grim smile.

"Which means she ain't aimin' to marry that crooked son of yours, Rance," observed old Chuckwalla thankfully.

"Yuh don't know he's crooked," retorted Rance.

"Mebby not; but his games is all shot to hell."

"Yuh mean that the gang has quit him, Chuckwalla?"

"Jist about, Rance. The Red Arrer is doin' the bulk of separation. The fool and his money ain't goin' near the Eagle these days."

"Chuckwalla, did you tell anybody about that deck?"

"Nossir. Didn't need to, Rance. There was other men at that table, and they had eyes in their heads. I tell yuh, Angel made a big mistake."

"Four thousand dollars would have busted him flat."

"Nobody hates a square gambler that goes busted."

"Do yuh reckon they're sayin' that Angel crooked me out of that twenty-five hundred?"

"Mebby not sayin' it, Rance."

"Believin' it, anyway."

"Somethin' like that. I look for Angel to sell out or close up pretty quick."

"He's got everythin' he owns tied up in the Eagle."

"Owns!" snorted Chuckwalla. "He didn't own anythin'. You was a big enough fool to give him a third of the Circle Spade stock. He didn't deserve anythin'. You paid him a puncher's salary since he was big enough to work, and then gave him that split of the stock. You're a fool, Rance."

"Mebby."

"Mebby! Yuh make me sick. I suppose you'll sell off half the stock you've got left and give the money to Lila."

"She wouldn't take it."

"No, I don't reckon she would. She always was an independent little critter. But Angel — well, he took anythin' that wasn't tied down. And you kinda favored him, Rance. I used to kinda wonder why it was, but since I heard what I did that night, I re'lize things. Blood is thicker'n water, after all is said and done."

Old Rance turned and looked at Chuckwalla wistfully.

"Wasn't I good to Lila?"

"Good? Shore yuh was. But yuh kinda favored Angel."

"I've tried to be good to both of 'em, Chuckwalla."

"I know yuh did, Rance. Hell, don't mind me."

"Yessir, I tried to be," wearily. "It was pretty rough in them days — when my wife died. She left me with the baby. I didn't know nothin' about babies, Chuckwalla. But I learned about 'em."

Old Rance smiled softly.

"Oh, I shore learned 'em. There wasn't many wimmin in that country, and them that was there had plenty to do without helpin' with mine. Packin' a six-gun in one hand and a diaper in the other. And then — I took another, Chuckwalla. Them two was almost of an age. They couldn't even talk English. Angel talked what sounded like a Cree language, while Lila runs pretty close to Navajo. I got so I could sabe both of 'em. It wasn't no fun. My God, I turned milkmaid. Fact. Got me a cow." Old Rance sighed deeply and shook his head. "She was a good cow."

"And yuh worked like hell to raise 'em — for this."

"Yeah. Well, I didn't have this in mind, Chuckwalla."

"Well, I reckon it'll turn out all right, Rance. You've played the game straight with the kids. But you're all through. They took the play away from yuh."

Chuckwalla got up from the steps and started to go into the house, but stopped. Angel was riding in through the old ranch-house gate. He dismounted at the porch, and stood with one foot on the lower step. Old Rance glanced up from under the brim of his sombrero.

"Howdy, Angel," he said.

"All right," replied Angel thoughtfully, looking at Chuckwalla. "You might as well stay, Chuckwalla. I want to talk with both of yuh."

Chuckwalla came back and leaned against a porch-post.

"I'm comin' right down to brass tacks," said Angel coldly. "What did you two say about me after that game the other day?"

41

Old Rance McCoy studied his son's face for several moments.

"Just what do yuh mean, Angel?"

"Chuckwalla swiped the deck of cards," said Angel slowly.

"I shore did!" snapped Chuckwalla. "And I found —"

"Wait a minute!" exclaimed Rance hoarsely. "This is for me to talk about, Chuckwalla. Now, what about the deck, Angel?"

"That's what I want to know," said Angel angrily. "Since that day I haven't had two-bits worth of play in my place. I've had to cut down to one man, besides the bartender; and if this keeps up I'll have to shut up the place. What I want to know is — what did you two say about me?"

Old Rance shook his head slowly.

"You're wrong, Angel; we didn't say a word to anybody. Was there somethin' crooked about yore dealin'?"

"Didn't say anythin', eh?" Angel ignored the question.

"There was other men around the table," reminded Chuckwalla. "They wasn't blind, young feller."

"You keep yore mouth out of this!" snapped Angel. "You took that deck over there on the sidewalk and — and —"

"And what?" demanded Chuckwalla. "You know what I done with it, Angel. Don't start gettin' tough with me, or I'll hang yore hide on the fence."

"Chuckwalla," said Rance mildly, "I'd like to talk with Angel alone."

"Shore thing."

Chuckwalla went into the house and began preparing a meal.

"Well, go ahead and talk," said Angel impatiently.

"You do the talkin'. You're more interested than I am."

"I'm sure interested enough," agreed Angel. "Do you think I made a crooked deal against you?"

"I watched pretty close, Angel."

"You would," sneered Angel. "You never trusted me very far."

"Too far — mebby. But that's outside the question. No matter what me and Chuckwalla thought — we kept still, Angel."

"Well, somebody talked," growled Angel. "My business is all shot — and it all happened that day. I haven't dealt a card in my place since. I know what they're sayin'. I'm no fool. They think I skinned you out of that money. They're sayin' that Angel McCoy was so crooked he skinned his own father. They say that you knew I skinned yuh. Oh, I heard it. No, I didn't hear it said, but I heard it was said."

"That ain't a — a good reputation, is it, Angel?"

"Reputation be damned! My business is —"

"Worth more than yore reputation, Angel?"

"Money talks."

"It does to some folks."

"Don't talk to me about reputation," said Angel hotly. "Yore own won't stand much, yuh know."

Old Rance blinked slowly, but the lines of his old face did not change. Perhaps his eyes clouded momentarily, but he was not looking at Angel.

"What do yuh want me to do?" he asked dully. "Why did yuh come out here, Angel?"

"I wanted to find out what you or Chuckwalla had said."

"We said nothin'."

Uh-huh."

It was evident that Angel did not believe this.

"You heard that Lila was goin' to teach school?"

Old Rance nodded. "Yeah, I heard she was."

"I wrote to Medicine Tree to find out more about her father — about Jim Stevens."

Old Rance turned slowly and looked at Angel, his eyes as hard as flint.

"Yuh did, eh? And what business was it of yours? What do you care about him?"

"Lila wanted to know more about him."

"Billy DuMond talked some more, eh?"

"No; not any more. He told me all he knew a long time ago. But that ain't got anythin' to do with my troubles. If this keeps up, I'm broke. I've got to prove I played on the square with you."

"How?"

"I'll be damned if I know."

"Did yuh, Angel?"

For several moments the young man looked at his father, turned on his heel, and went back to his horse.

"I suppose it's the proper thing to do — to squawk about a crooked deal when yuh lose a few dollars," he said, as he mounted his horse.

Old Rance watched him ride away. Old Chuckwalla came to the doorway, carrying a skillet in his hand, and looked down the road, where a cloud of dust showed the swift passing of the horse and rider.

"And I suppose you're feelin' sorry for *him*," said Chuckwalla.

Rance nodded slowly, but did not look around.

"Blood's a hell of a lot thicker'n water; but if he was my son, I'd kick the seat of his pants up so high that they'd tilt his hat forward."

"You never had a son, didja, Chuckwalla?"

"No, thank God!"

"Amen," said old Rance piously.

"Is that supposed to be a smart remark?" asked Chuckwalla.

"No; I just thought it fit the case, Chuckwalla. If yuh never had a son, yuh ain't fit to pass judgment on a father."

I suppose there's a lot of truth in that remark. But I know Angel pretty well, Rance. By golly, I'm glad Lila's got a job. She'll make good. And she won't demand no split of yore money, old-timer. There's a girl!"

"Yeah," muttered Rance. "She's independent. But I — I wish she'd stay here and be independent."

CHAPTER
SIX

Lila

The fall term of school was about ready to start, and Lila was offered her board and room with the Parker family. Jim Parker was proprietor of the Red Arrow General Merchandise Store, and was also one of the trustees of the school.

Jim Parker was a big, bluff, self-opinionated sort of person, while Mrs. Parker was a little old lady at forty, whose sole aim in life was to take care of their two children and make Jim comfortable. She welcomed Lila for companionship, and Jim welcomed her for what added instructions she might impart to his offspring.

Angel did not like the idea of Lila living with the Parker family, because of the fact that he and Jim Parker had never been friends. Angel had never mentioned marriage to Lila since the day they had talked with Billy DuMond. In fact, he had seen little of her.

No one had asked Lila why she had left the Circle Spade, and it seemed that many thought it was because she was merely starting out to make her own way in the world. No hint of the suspicions against Angel McCoy had come to her ears. She did not know that Angel had written to the sheriff of Medicine Tree, seeking information of what had happened to Jim Stevens years ago.

Quite a number of the Red Arrow cowboys had looked with favor upon Lila McCoy, but none of them had summoned up enough nerve to visit her at Parker's home, except Slim Caldwell, the sheriff. He had known Lila for years, and came to congratulate her on her new job. It took him from eight o'clock to midnight to offer his congratulations, much to the amusement of Jim Parker, who sat with them all that time in the living-room. Slim resolved to get even with Jim at the first opportunity. And Jim Parker added insult to injury when he told Chuck Ring about it.

Chuck's version was rather wonderful.

"And there they sat, all night long; Lila asleep in her chair, and Slim and Jim glarin' at each other until about five o'clock in the mornin', when Slim went to sleep. Jim wakes Lila up and she goes to her room, and Jim goes to bed. Slim didn't wake up until Mrs. Parker starts gettin' breakfast, and then he sneaks out."

But he came again, and though nobody knew what had happened, Jim Parker let Lila and Slim strictly alone.

All of which did not set so well with Angel McCoy. He was in the proper frame of mind to take Chuck's version without reservations. Things were going worse with Angel. He had kept only one dealer, and was thinking seriously of cutting him off the payroll of the Eagle.

And it was about this time that Lila heard Jim Parker talking to another man about Angel McCoy. They were discussing the business at the Eagle, and Parker remarked that Angel had no one to blame except himself.

"You know what they're sayin'," said Parker. "He took twenty-five hundred away from old Rance McCoy, and some of the boys say it was a crooked deal. I never heard the old man say a word about it — but he wouldn't."

"I guess it was a crooked deal all right," agreed the other man. "Doesn't seem to be any secret."

Lila went to her room to think it over. Angel a thief! Dealt a crooked game to beat his own father! And old Rance McCoy had given him the money to buy out that gambling-house. She went downstairs and talked to Mrs. Parker, trying to find out what she knew about it.

"Yes, I heard about it," admitted Mrs. Parker. "I didn't want to say anything about it, Lila. Angel has made a lot of enemies over it, and has practically ruined his business."

"But he surely wouldn't steal from his father, Mrs. Parker."

"Honey, a gambler don't recognize relationship. Angel always was a queer sort of a boy — rather cold-blooded. I don't care if he is your brother —"

"But he isn't," said Lila softly. "Oh, I don't think there is any use of keeping it a secret. That was why I left the Circle Spade ranch. Haven't you wondered?"

"A little — yes. Others have wondered, too. But I supposed it was merely because you wanted to earn your own living."

"Rance McCoy is not my father, Mrs. Parker. He — he shot my father when I was a baby. I don't know why, but he adopted me and gave me his name. Angel and I are no relation. My father was named Stevens."

"Well, heavens above! Can you imagine that? Honey, that's like something you read about. A-a-a-w, don't cry about it! You can't help it, can you? Pshaw! Did Rance McCoy tell you?"

Lila shook her head quickly her lips trembling.

"A-Angel told me. Rance McCoy didn't deny it."

"Well." Mrs. Parker thought it over carefully. "Well, I don't think that it's so bad. Rance took care of you and gave you an education. You've got to give him credit for that."

"Oh, I do give him credit. But I'll pay him back for all that."

"If I know anything about Rance McCoy, he ain't looking for pay. And it'll take you a mighty long time to ever earn enough to pay him back."

The next day was payday on some of the ranches, and, being Saturday, nearly all the cattlemen came to town. The Red Arrow Saloon was crowded with chap-clad gentry all day. Some of the boys would drop in at the Eagle, buy a round of drinks and go out, none of them offering to buck the games.

Jim Langley came in from the JML, bringing Jess Fohl and "Roper" Briggs, two of his cowboys. Langley was a well-built, dark-faced man, whose hair was sprinkled with gray. He was not a mixer, and seldom came to town. Chuck Ring swore that Langley had a "past."

"Don't talk much," observed Chuck wisely. "Does a lot of thinkin'. And he packs his gun too handy for a feller that's easy in the mind."

But there was nothing reticent about Fohl and Briggs. They were a tough pair, and they wanted it understood. Both were less than thirty years of age. Fohl was bow-legged, his head typically Prussian. Briggs was wry-necked, had little chin, and a pair of tiny blue eyes, which were so round that it gave one the feeling that here was a piece of human taxidermy in which the workman had inserted bird-eyes in a human head.

These three men had a drink at the Eagle, sized up the place curiously, and went over to the Red Arrow to find out the why-for of the boycott on the Eagle. And they found out. Several of the boys were just drunk enough to speak plain about Angel McCoy. Billy DuMond was there, drinking plenty, but keeping an eye on the front door and keeping his gun handy.

The lamps were already lighted when Langley and his two men came to the Red Arrow. The games were crowded.

"Well, is it true that Angel crooked the old man out of twenty-five hundred?" queried Langley, talking to those at the bar.

"He did!" said DuMond emphatically. "Not that I give a damn about it, yuh understand. Me and old McCoy ain't been friends for years, and I hope I live long enough to tip over his tombstone, but it was a dirty deal. Angel's a crook if there ever was one."

DuMond hammered on the bar with his glass and indicated to the bartender that they would drink again.

"Old Rance was in town to-day," offered Eddie Marsh, one of the 77 punchers. "I seen him at the bank."

"Thasso?" DuMond cleared his throat harshly. "Mebby he knowed I was comin' in, and that's why he pulled out."

"You're crazy," declared Butch Reimer. "He'd fill you full of lead before yuh could reach to yore gun."

"Like hell!" flared DuMond. "He ain't so fast. You gimme an even break with that old hound, and I'll — I'll —"

DuMond's voice trailed off into space. He was staring at the back-bar mirror as though hypnotized. Butch Reimer leaned forward, staring into the mirror too. Directly behind them stood old Rance McCoy, his stony old eyes looking at them in the mirror. DuMond choked softly. His elbows were on the top of the bar, and it seemed that he was unable to lift them off.

Langley turned and looked at the old man.

"Hyah, Rance," he said, smiling. "Long time I no see yuh."

But the old man's eyes did not shift.

"Turn around, DuMond," he said softly.

DuMond whined deep in his throat, a sort of a strangle. With a supreme effort he drew his elbows off the bar and turned around, his hands held almost shoulder-high. He blinked at old man McCoy painfully.

51

The old man had his hands resting on his hips, his head thrust forward.

"Let yore hands down, DuMond."

"No," said DuMond hollowly. "I — I — what did yuh say, McCoy?"

"Yuh can't draw from up there, DuMond. Let yore hands down to yore waist. I'm givin' yuh that even break yuh wanted."

"Even break?" DuMond's eyes shifted and he looked around at the hazy faces of the many men in the place. There was nobody directly behind McCoy. DuMond's eyes were full of tears, as though he had been looking at a bright light.

"Yuh wanted an even break, yuh said," reminded old Rance evenly.

"Not me," said DuMond in a strained voice. "Oh, not me, McCoy. What I said was —"

DuMond swallowed heavily, but was unable to go ahead with his explanation. Rance McCoy moved slowly ahead until he stood within a foot of the shrinking DuMond. Then he deliberately slapped DuMond across the mouth, knocking him back against the bar. But DuMond did not drop his right hand. His left slowly went to his lips and he stood there, leaning back against the bar, the back of his left hand held tightly against his lips, as though to ward off a blow. There was a crimson trickle down his stubbled chin below the protecting hand.

"Get out of here," commanded Rance McCoy, pointing toward the open door. "Get out of here, you pup; I want to talk to men."

And DuMond went — still holding his right hand high, his left hand guarding his bruised lips.

Old Rance watched him leave the place before he turned to the men who had seen him humiliate Billy DuMond. Then he stepped in against the bar and turned to face them. His hard old eyes looked from face to face, as he said:

"I know what's been said about the Eagle. You've heard that Angel McCoy is a crooked gambler and that he stole a lot of money from me. That's a damned lie, and the man who says it is a liar!"

No one contradicted him. He gave them plenty of time. Then —

"I've played cards before a lot of yuh was born, and I know a crooked deal. It's none of my business where yuh lose yore money, but I jist wanted to tell yuh that I'm goin' to play mine at the Eagle."

Then he surged away from the bar and walked from the place. The room had been silent from the first word he had spoken to Billy DuMond, and no one spoke until he had left the place, but now they all tried to talk at once.

Langley and Butch Reimer left the bar together and went across the street, followed by nearly every man in the Red Arrow, impelled by curiosity.

But Angel McCoy was not there; he was sitting on the steps of Jim Parker's home, trying to argue Lila into agreeing to marry him. But all his arguments were fruitless.

"Well, yuh can't teach school all your life," he declared.

"I can if I want to, Angel."

"Oh, I suppose yuh can. Mebby you was foolish to quit the old man the way yuh did. You'll never get anythin' more out of him. I got my share, I'll tell yuh that. I got more than you'll ever get."

"I have no gambling game to entice him," said Lila meaningly.

Angel got quickly to his feet.

"So yuh heard about that little deal, eh?" angrily. "That's why yuh act so cool, is it? What is there about it to bother you, I'd like to know? Who told yuh about it?"

"It doesn't seem to be any secret, Angel."

"Secret! Ha, ha, ha, ha, ha! No, I guess not."

"It doesn't seem to amuse any one, except you, Angel."

"No?" Angel moved closer to her in the dark. "Yuh don't see anythin' to laugh about, eh? Well, I don't either. I'm not laughing because it's funny. Every cent I own is tied up in that saloon. And these hypocrites have boycotted me. They don't know it was a crooked deal. Old Rance McCoy came in there to beat me. He drew twenty-five hundred from the bank to try and break me. But he failed. I know my own game. I'm not in that business to let anybody break me. I went into it to make easy money."

"But he is your father, Angel."

"What of it? You think blood is thicker than water, eh? Not in my business. Everythin' is grist that comes to my mill. They think I'm crooked, eh? I'll sell out here and go to another place. You come with me and I'll see that yuh wear diamonds, Lila. I can make more money than yuh ever seen. Think it over. You wasn't born to teach school, or marry a forty-a-month puncher."

"Thank you, Angel."

"What for? I mean every word of it. Don't let old Rance McCoy worry yuh."

"Does he think you played a crooked game?"

"What if he does?"

"Don't you want the respect of your father, Angel?"

"What good will it do me? The respect of Rance McCoy!"

"You are a queer son, Angel."

"Am I? Well, I'm what I am — and I'm satisfied."

"Satisfied to be known as a cheat?"

Angel laughed angrily.

"Who cares? Nobody can prove I cheated him."

"You can, Angel; and you must have a conscience."

"Not a damned bit! That's somethin' that wasn't in the McCoy family; so where could I inherit it? I don't mind tellin' you that if I had played a square game, I'd be broke now. That ain't admittin' anythin', is it? Ha, ha, ha, ha, ha! Well, you think it over, Lila. It's the difference between wearin' diamonds and — and what you're goin' to do."

Angel walked away from her, and she heard the rusty hinges of the old gate creak behind him. She shivered slightly and drew the pale blue shawl closer around her shoulders. She had not seen Rance McCoy since she had left the ranch, and in spite of her prejudice there was an ache in her heart for the old man who had raised her. He had been so glad to see her when she came back from the East, after five years of school. He had not said much, but she could see the pleasure and happiness in his eyes as he held her off at arm's length and looked her over.

And she had been glad to see Angel. Somehow she had forgotten that Angel had been nicknamed for the same reason that a fat cowboy was usually known as "Slim." He was a handsome man now, the handsomest man she had ever met; and he had told her that he loved her, almost in the same breath that he had told her she was not his sister. His whirlwind method had left her breathless, and she could not remember now just what she had told him.

But he was still the same Angel McCoy, cold-blooded, headstrong, sarcastic. She remembered one Sunday when Rance had taken them to Sunday School at Red Arrow. Angel was about ten years old. The lesson had made a strong impression on him, and late that afternoon one of the cowboys had found him out behind the stable, crucifying a cat against the corner of the corral fence.

Old Rance did not whip him. Lila could not remember that Rance had ever whipped Angel. He had whipped her. Somehow, she held that against him now. He would not whip his own child. He had never whipped her very hard, but it was the humiliation more than the actual pain.

She remembered that old Rance had whipped a cowboy who had slapped Angel. It was nearly a gun-fight. Angel had cut the strings all off the cowboy's saddle and was using them to braid into a quirt for himself. Old Rance whipped the cowboy, and then paid a saddle-maker to put the strings back on the saddle again.

He had always protected Angel. She had heard Angel talking back to him one day, and old Rance had said:

"All right, son. Some day you'll be twenty-one. Until that time, you're a kid. When you're twenty-one, you'll be a man — and I'd shoot a man for sayin' what you've just said to me. I don't quarrel with kids, but just remember what I said."

And she had seen Rance McCoy kill a man. Lila was twelve at the time. It was over a branding deal, she remembered. The men were all standing around the corral gate, and she had climbed halfway up the fence near them. She remembered that one of the men was standing apart from the rest, and his face was very white. Then she heard him say:

"McCoy, you're a liar!"

There were two shots fired, spaced less than a second apart, and she saw this man crumple up and fall on his face. It was such a shock that she nearly fell off the fence. Then some one picked her off the fence, and she turned her head to see it was Rance McCoy. He said to the men:

"You saw and heard it all, boys. Better get the sheriff and tell him about it."

Then he had carried her to the house and told her to run along and play. It was the first time he had ever picked her up since she could remember. And she had rather resented it, because she was twelve years of age.

It was growing cool out there on the porch, so she went into the house and sat down to read. Mrs. Parker was busy upstairs and Jim Parker had not come in from the store.

CHAPTER
SEVEN

Rance Wins Out

Angel McCoy went straight back to the Eagle. There were men on the porch of the saloon, and he wondered at the number of them. Rather breathlessly he shoved his way into the place and looked around. There were at least thirty men in the saloon, and quite a number of them were crowded around the black-jack layout. There were no players at any of the other tables, because there were no dealers. The bartender was working at top speed.

Wonderingly Angel worked his way around to the black-jack table, and stopped against the wall. Old Rance McCoy and three other men were playing. Near the end of the table stood Chuckwalla Ike, puffing industriously on a frayed-out cigar, closely watching the dealer.

Old Rance was betting with hundred-dollar bills, and as Angel watched him he lost five in quick succession. In his left hand he clutched a huge roll of currency, from which he stripped off bill after bill.

"Let's make it worth while," said old Rance. "Here's five hundred."

Angel watched the old man win the bet. The dealer's eyes flashed quickly around the crowd, and he saw Angel.

"Let it ride," said the old man. "Why don't some of yuh buy into this game? I don't want to hog all of it."

Several of the cattlemen made small bets, as Angel moved around behind the dealer.

"There's a hundred-dollar limit, gents," said Angel easily.

Old Rance looked at Angel quizzically.

"Hundred dollars, eh?" he queried. "That's too slow."

"It's shore too heavy for me," laughed Jim Langley. "I'm limited to five-dollar bets myself. Rance is the only millionaire around here."

Old Rance slowly pocketed the money, after throwing a hundred dollars on the table, and the deal went on. Angel backed away and went around to the stud-poker table, where he laid out the chips and broke open a new deck of cards. The table filled in a few moments. In the larger houses there is a dealer, who merely does the dealing and takes care of the rake-off for the house, but in a place like the Eagle the dealer takes an active part in the game, passing the buck each time to indicate which player is to be dealt to first.

There was no limit in the stud game. Chips ran according to color, from twenty-five cents to ten dollars. The cowboys played a cautious game. A forty-dollar pay check would not last long in a game of that kind unless the player either played in luck or used good judgment.

Old Rance won consistently. Hundred after hundred went to swell the roll of bills in his pocket. The rest of the players merely piked along, causing the dealer little concern. "Rance is a thousand to the good," announced a cowboy, who had come from the black-jack layout to look at the poker game.

Angel bit the corner of his lip and blinked at his cards. He could ill afford to lose a thousand, and he knew the old man was on a betting spree. Ten minutes later the dealer came and spoke softly to him:

"Eighteen hundred to the bad, Angel; and I'm out of money."

"Close the game," said Angel harshly.

A poker-player drew out of the game, and old Rance took his place. He threw a hundred-dollar bill across to Angel.

"Table stakes, Angel?" he asked.

"Table stakes," growled Angel, meaning that a player could bet only the amount of money in front of him.

The old man drew out his enormous roll of money and placed it beside his chips. Angel eyed the roll closely. There were thousands in that roll. He did not know that old Rance had drawn every cent of money he had on deposit in the bank; a total of seventy-five hundred.

Old Rance's first open card was the ace of spades. He looked at it and laughed across the table at Angel. It was the best card in sight, and the old man threw ten yellow chips — one hundred dollars' worth — into the pot.

61

The players promptly passed. None of them felt like taking a chance, even with only two cards dealt in each hand. Angel sneered openly and covered the bet. He realized that the old man was aiming the bet at him. Angel had a queen buried and a ten-spot in sight.

The next two cards showed a king for Rance and another ten for Angel.

"Pair of tens bet a hundred," said Angel.

"Make it two hundred," replied Rance, taking the money off his roll. Angel acquiesced, after considering another raise.

The next two cards showed another ace to Rance and a queen for Angel. This gave Rance two aces in sight and an ace in the hole, while Angel's two tens and a queen in sight gave him queens and tens. Rance promptly bet a hundred dollars, and Angel just as promptly boosted it a hundred.

Rance grew thoughtful, and after due deliberation he raised the bet another hundred. Angel called. A gasp went up when Rance drew another ace, and Angel a ten.

"Three aces bets," drawled Angel.

Old Rance made a motion as though to turn over his buried card, but hesitated and checked the bet. Angel bet two hundred dollars — twenty yellow chips.

Rance laughed softly, eying Angel's three tens and the queen.

"Up three hundred," he said softly, as he deliberately peeled off more bills.

It was Angel's turn to be thoughtful. He had a ten-full on queens. Those three aces worried him, but he was too deep in the pot to stop now. Slowly he counted off fifty of the yellow chips, fingering them softly. Then he shoved them into the center of the table.

"Up two hundred," he said coldly.

Old Rance eyed Angel coldly, as he peeled off the amount of the raise and tossed it to the center. He counted off three hundred more and added it to the huge pile of money and yellow chips.

"Three hundred more?" asked Angel hoarsely.

Old Rance did not reply; he did not need to. Angel's hand trembled as he counted out the required amount in chips.

"Just callin' me?" queried Rance.

"Looks like it, don't it?" growled Angel.

Old Rance turned over his fourth ace. He had won eighteen hundred dollars in one hand. Angel looked dumbly at him, as he returned the money to his roll, and stacked the piles of yellow chips. Old Rance had already won thirty-six hundred dollars from Angel. But the evening was young.

Angel spoke to the dealer, who stood behind him:

"Bring me some yellow chips."

And when the man came with the chips he said to him:

"Open the black-jack game, Bud; it looks like a big night."

Angel was game. He didn't have enough cash to redeem those yellow chips. He had only had a trifle over three thousand in cash to start the evening play, and there was less than a thousand dollars of his money left in the bank. But Angel was a gambler, and he had no intention of letting the old man get away with all that money.

There was nothing spectacular about the next hand. Rance dropped out after the second card, and Jim Langley won the pot. But on the next hand old Rance called a five-dollar bet by Jess Fohl, and boosted it a hundred.

"Tryin' to run everybody out?" queried Fohl.

"A runner ain't got no business in this game, Jess."

He looked straight at Angel, who flushed hotly and called the bet. The rest of the players dropped out. Fohl cursed over the loss of his money. He had a pair of sevens, back-to-back, and didn't want to drop; but the hundred was more than he could stand.

In sight, Rance had a six, and Angel had a five. Angel reasoned that Rance must have a six in the hole, in order to raise the bet. Rance drew an ace, while Angel drew a nine. It cost Angel another hundred to draw, but he did not raise.

Angel drew a six the next time, and Rance drew a trey. It was Rance's bet, but he checked it to Angel, who promptly bet a hundred, and Rance merely called the bet. The next two cards showed a nine to Rance and a four to Angel.

Neither player had a pair in sight.

"Ace, nine bets," droned Angel, and Rance promptly bet the usual hundred dollars, and Angel passed. He turned over the ace he had buried, and shut his lips angrily when old Rance disclosed a deuce of clubs. Angel's ace, nine, six, five would have beaten Rance's ace, nine, six, trey.

"Of all the damned fool bettin'!" exclaimed Chuckwalla, who was still trying to smoke that frayed-out cigar. "Winnin' over three hundred dollars on ace high."

"Nerve," corrected old Rance easily.

"Nerve!" sneered Angel. "You raised that first bet with a deuce in the hole and a six exposed. You're crazy."

"Just nerve," said Rance coldly. "Somethin' you ain't got."

"You think I ain't?"

Old Rance leaned across the table, looking steadily at his son.

"How much nerve have yuh got, Angel?"

"I've got enough."

"I wonder if yuh have. I've got about thirty-nine hundred of yore money right now, Angel. Have yuh got nerve enough to bet me another thirty-nine hundred that I don't get the first ace off the deck?"

Angel stared at him, his eyes half-closed. Thirty-nine hundred more. Still, luck might be with him this time. It was a chance to win back all he'd lost.

"Neither of us will deal," said Rance softly. "We'll let Jim Langley deal to us, and we'll cut to see who gets the first card."

"All right," said Angel, trying to make his voice sound calm.

Rance won the cut, and leaned back indifferently while Jim Langley shuffled the deck. Angel cut the cards first, and when Langley presented the cards to Rance, he waived the right to cut them.

"Are yuh all ready?" asked Langley nervously.

"Let 'em go," said Angel.

"By God, an ace!" exploded Chuckwalla.

It was the first card off the deck — the ace of spades. Jim Langley slowly replaced the deck on the table and stepped back. Angel stared at the card, licked his dry lips, and finally shrugged his shoulders. Seventy-eight hundred dollars! He looked at his father, who was leaning one elbow on the table, calmly counting the yellow chips.

"You got enough?" asked Angel hoarsely.

"Yeah," said Rance. He stacked the chips and shoved them over to Angel, who mechanically counted them before placing them in the rack.

"Is this game goin' ahead?" asked Langley.

"In a few minutes," said Angel. He looked at his father, as he got to his feet.

"Come on and I'll cash yuh in," he said. The old man nodded and they went to the rear of the saloon, entering Angel's private room.

Angel shut the door and leaned back against it, while the old man stood near the center, looking at him.

"You're broke, eh?" said Rance coldly.

"Yeah, I'm broke," admitted Angel. "I ain't got enough money to keep my games open. I've got about nine hundred in the bank."

"And you owe me about six thousand dollars," said Rance.

"Yeah."

Old Rance studied the face of his son for several moments.

"Yuh stole an ace the other day, Angel."

"Well?" Angel did not deny it.

"Everybody knows it," said Rance softly. "It ruined yore business. I brought the business back for yuh, and now yuh ain't got enough money to keep it rollin'. Here!"

He drew out his roll of bills, stripped off the eighteen hundred he had won at the black-jack game, and gave it to the wondering Angel.

"Now," said Rance coldly, "give me yore I.O.U. for the full seventy-eight hundred."

Angel's eyes brightened quickly.

"You mean you'll take my I.O.U. for that —"

"I always was a fool," said the old man bitterly. "Go ahead and write it out."

Angel sat down at his table and quickly wrote out the I.O.U., which the old man accepted.

"Go back to yore games," said old Rance. "And see if yuh can't deal fair."

They went back into the saloon and Angel opened the poker game again. Old Rance went to the bar with Chuckwalla, and had a drink. The old man had had several drinks before the game, and now he piled in several more. Chuckwalla held the smudging cigar in his gnarled fingers and tossed down drink after drink.

The black-jack game playing dwindled to nothing, and the dealer closed the game until some customers showed up. In the meantime he went across the street and up to the corner to the post-office.

Old Rance left the bar and went over to the poker table; not with any intention of playing again, but

67

merely drawn by the fascination of the game. In a few minutes the dealer came back, handing Angel a letter as he came past the table. Angel glanced at the postmark on the letter. It was from Medicine Tree.

Jim Langley dropped out of the game and old Rance took his chair. He indicated with a shake of his head that he did not wish to play. Angel signaled to the dealer to take his place, and as soon as the substitution was made, he went over to the end of the bar, tore open the envelope, and began reading the letter.

Jim Parker closed his store at nine o'clock and went home. He had heard that Rance McCoy was bucking the game in the Eagle, plunging heavily on the black-jack game. But Parker was too tired to go over and see just what was going on.

Lila was in her room, which adjoined the Parkers' bedroom, reading, when Jim Parker and his wife came up to bed, and she heard them discussing what Parker had heard.

"Oh, the Eagle is filled up, they tell me," said Parker. "I didn't go over. One of the boys said that old Rance had a roll of bills that would choke a horse, and he's bettin' 'em high. What Angel will do to him will be plenty."

"Hasn't Rance any sense at all?" queried Mrs. Parker.

"Oh, I don't know," replied Parker sleepily. "Maybe he don't know that Angel is a crooked dealer. He wouldn't expect his own son to steal from him, would he? I'm glad tomorrow is Sunday."

"Somebody ought to warn old Rance," said Mrs. Parker.

"Well, don't try it, my dear. It's none of our business. If he wants to go against a crooked deal — let him go."

"How much money do you suppose he'll lose, Jim?"

"Who — Rance? All he's got. No, I'm not jokin'. Rance is a gambler, and he'll bet as long as he's got a cent."

Lila got to her feet and picked up the pale blue shawl. She could go downstairs without passing the Parkers' room; so she tiptoed softly down, let herself out through the front door, which was never kept locked, and went quickly out to the street.

It did not take her long to reach the Eagle Saloon. Some cowboys stared at her as she came into the lights, but she paid no attention to them. A cowboy was at the bar, singing a plaintive melody in a drunken tenor, and there was a babel of voices, the clatter of poker chips.

Angel was back in the game again. She could see the back of Rance McCoy's grizzled old head, his sombrero tilted forward to shield his eyes. The room was full of tobacco-smoke. Chuckwalla Ike saw her first. He blinked foolishly and stumbled toward her, trying to tell her to get out of there, but she eluded him and came in behind old Rance, putting a hand on his shoulder.

Angel was dealing, but halted quickly. Every one in the room was staring at her. Old Rance turned his head and looked up at her white face, a puzzled expression in his eyes.

"What do yuh want, Lila?" he asked.

"Don't play against him," she said hoarsely, pointing at Angel. "Please don't. He admitted that he dealt crooked to you. He's a cheat. He — he told me he did."

The room was silent. Angel's face flushed hotly and he surged to his feet, kicking back his chair.

"That's a lie!" he hurled at her. "I never told yuh any such a thing. You get out of here! This is no place for you."

Lila faced him defiantly.

"I came to tell Rance McCoy what you did to him, Angel. If he wants to play now — all right."

"You came to warn him, eh?" sneered Angel. "Playin' politics, are yuh? Tryin' to get in good with the old man. Lemme tell yuh somethin' about yourself. I just got a letter tonight. Yore father was a thief — a bank-robber! He was killed —"

Old Rance sprang out of his chair and leaned across the table toward Angel.

"Shut up, you dirty pup!" he gritted. "Give me that letter!"

"What if I won't?" snapped Angel.

"Then I'll take it off yore dead carcass."

The old man had swayed sideways and his right elbow was bent slightly. The men behind Angel sagged aside quickly.

"It's in yore coat pocket," said Rance warningly.

Slowly Angel reached into his pocket, took out the letter, and flung it down in front of his father. Quickly the old man tore it into small pieces, flinging them aside with a flip of his wrist.

70

The men were staring at old Rance, wondering what it was all about. They did not know what Angel knew about Lila's parentage, and as far as they were concerned, they thought Angel was accusing old Rance of being these things.

Old Rance reached back and took Lila by the arm.

"It's all right," he said brokenly. "Yuh can't expect it to always work out jist right. C'mon, Lila."

They walked out together, the crowd staring after them. Angel's face was a little more white than usual as he dropped back into his chair, ready to resume the game. But the players cashed in their chips and went out, until no one remained in the place, except Angel, the other dealer, and the bartender.

Rance walked as far as the gate of the Parker home with Lila. Neither of them said anything until they reached the gate, when Lila said:

"Oh, I'm sorry it happened. I simply had to tell you. But I — I guess I forgot he was your own son."

"That's all right, Lila; it was thoughtful of yuh to even think of me."

"But that letter —" faltered Lila. "What letter was it?"

"I dunno," slowly. "Forget it."

"But he — he said my father was a thief and a bank-robber."

Old Rance was silent for several moments.

"I don't reckon Angel got the truth of the matter," he said softly. "You forget it, Lila. Good-night."

He turned and faded out in the darkness, going back to the main street. The bulk of the crowd had gone back to the Red Arrow, and there was much speculation regarding what had happened at the Eagle.

Old Chuckwalla Ike had gone back there with the crowd, and was drinking prodigious quantities of raw liquor. One of the men asked him what Angel had meant by telling the girl what he did. But Chuckwalla swore he didn't know.

"Angel's crazy," he declared. "Allus been crazy. Never did have the sense that God gave geese in Ireland."

"Well, he shore got trimmed," declared Jim Langley. "Think of dealin' first ace for five thousand! I figure old Rance won pretty close to eight thousand from Angel; and if Angel can pay him off, I'm an Eskimo in Florida."

"Old Rance owns the Eagle right now," stated another. "He shore paid Angel for his crooked dealin'."

Old Chuckwalla got pretty drunk before he left the Red Arrow and went on a hunt for old Rance. The Eagle was dark. Chuckwalla managed to paw his way along the hitch-rack and to locate his horse. It was only after several tries that he was able to get into the saddle. Once he went all the way over the horse, but had presence of mind enough to cling to the reins.

"Shore gettin' active in m' old age," he told himself as he tried to get his foot out of his hat. "Ain't many men of my age that can leap plumb over a bronc in the dark."

He finally got seated and rode out of town, swaying in his saddle, and trying to sing. It was about eleven o'clock when he reached the Circle Spade. By this time he was sober enough to unsaddle his horse, turn it loose in a corral, and go up to the ranch-house, where he went to bed. His horse had picked up a small stone in the frog of its right front foot, and was limping badly, but Chuckwalla didn't know it.

CHAPTER
EIGHT

The Overland Makes an Unexpected Stop

It was near midnight when the Overland train, traveling north, came in sight of Curlew Spur. The Overland did not stop at Curlew Spur, nor did it stop at Red Arrow except on a flag, but this night, from beside the track at Curlew Spur, blinked a tiny red light.

It was something that no engineer would ignore. The big passenger train, roaring up through the Red Arrow Valley, suddenly slackened speed, and the engineer swore inwardly at the signal that would put him off his schedule.

The train ground to a stop, with the pilot of the engine just past the red lantern, which was sitting on a block of wood. There was no one in sight. On the right-hand side of the train was the shadowy bulk of the loading-pens. On the other side was nothing but open country. Here the track ran straight for nearly a mile, and as far as the powerful headlight bored out through the night, the track was open.

The engineer swung down from his cab and walked over to the lantern, where he was joined in a few minutes by the conductor and one of the brakemen. It was a common lantern, with an old red bandanna handkerchief wrapped around it.

"What's it all about?" asked the conductor angrily. He was a portly individual, inclined to wheeze heavily.

"I dunno," grunted the engineer. "You see it, don't you?"

The conductor picked up the lantern, turning it slowly in his hands.

"Some smart jigger playing a joke," decided the brakeman. "Maybe some bo flagged us down for a ride."

"I'd like to get my hands on him!" snapped the engineer.

The brakeman turned to the conductor.

"You go down this side and I'll go down the other. Unless he's on top, we'll find him."

The brakeman circled the engine and walked down the other side of the train, flashing his lantern beneath the trucks of the coaches, but without any success. He and the portly conductor met on the right-hand side of the train.

"Nobody in sight," said the brakeman wearily. "Might as well high-ball, Charley."

The engineer had climbed back into his cab, and he saw one of the men signal him to go ahead. It was slightly upgrade, and the staccato exhaust echoed across the hills as the big drivers spinned ahead of the sand stream. Then the drivers gripped heavily and the engine surged ahead.

They had proceeded about a hundred yards, when the fireman, looking back toward the rear, noticed that the lights of the rear coach were getting farther away all the time.

He turned quickly and yelled at the engineer:

"Hey! We're broke in two, Frank!"

But before the engineer could grasp the import of his words a man was standing in the gangway behind them, covering them with a heavy six-shooter. The man was masked with a black cloth that covered all of his head and neck. The engineer started to retard the throttle.

"Pull her open!" snapped the masked man. "Git back there on yore seat and look ahead."

The fireman obeyed. There was nothing else for him to do. For about a mile and a half the engineer ran at about twenty-five miles per hour.

"Cut her down," ordered the masked man. They were entering a deep cut, where the road turned sharply to the left.

"Slow down and stop here at the end of the cut."

The man was brisk and business-like, wasting no words. The engine slowed and stopped, and the engineer waited for the next order.

"Both of yuh go down ahead of me. No funny business. I'm not takin' any chances."

The engine crew descended, and close on their heels came the masked man. It was then that they realized that the express car was still attached to the engine.

"March back to the express car — single-file. Remember it's light enough for good shootin'."

They went back along the track, stumbling over stones and tie-ends, until they were at the door of the car.

"You know this messenger?" asked the bandit.

"I don't," said the engineer.

"All right. Knock on the door, tell him who yuh are, and that if he don't open the door, I'll blow it open. I'll give him just five seconds to make up his mind. I'm ready to do the job up right."

The engineer hammered heavily on the door and was greeted by an instant response. The door rolled open and a sleepy-eyed messenger stared out at them. He was looking down into the muzzle of a heavy revolver.

"Slip yore gun loose and drop it," he ordered.

The messenger drew out his gun and dropped it on the car floor. The bandit motioned for the engineer and fireman to climb into the car, but before they were both inside, the bandit swung up the other side and was facing them.

"I — I was asleep," faltered the messenger. "Thought we'd made a stop at Red Arrow."

"Lucky thing yuh did," growled the bandit. "Open yore safe."

The messenger shook his head.

"I can't unlock it."

"All right."

The bandit kicked the messenger's revolver toward the upper end of the car.

"Three of yuh set on that trunk," he ordered. After they were perched together on a sample trunk, he went over to the through safe and proceeded to set his explosives. He had the light behind him; so they were unable to see just how he prepared the charge. It was ready inside of twenty seconds.

"Get behind those trunks," he said, and they lost no time.

On the wall near him hung the messenger's sawed-off shotgun, and he took it off the wall, pumped out the cartridges, and tossed the gun aside, before he lighted the short fuse and stepped farther back against the wall.

The car jarred heavily from the explosion, and a gust of smoke billowed toward the open doorway. Before the three men dared lift their heads, the bandit was squatting at the wrecked safe, facing them, as he looted it of package and canvas sack. He stuffed the packages in his pocket and inside his shirt, while the three men choked in the fumes of nitroglycerine.

Then the bandit got quickly to his feet and stepped to the doorway. For a moment he looked back at the three men before he dropped to the ground.

"Can you beat that?" choked the messenger. "The nerve of the devil!" He choked from the smoke, stooped quickly and swept up his revolver. Running to the door of the car, he leaned out.

From out in the darkness came a streak of flame and a bullet struck the opposite side of the doorway. As fast as he could pull the trigger the messenger sent six shots into the darkness.

But there was no reply from the bandit. It was a full minute before any of them would dare to venture to the open doorway. But everything was serene.

"How much was in the safe?" asked the engineer.

"I don't know — plenty. Let's go."

As quickly as possible they backed to the spur, where they picked up the rest of the train. The wheezy conductor was almost incoherent, acting as though the engineer was personally to blame for running away without the rest of the train.

They did not need a flag to stop them at Red Arrow. The lethargic telegraph operator woke up and fairly burned up the wires, while another man ran down the street to the sheriff's office, where he hammered on the door.

"Git away fr-rom there, ye dr-r-runken bum!" wailed the sleepy voice of Scotty McKay. "Don't ye know a jail when ye see one?"

"The Overland train has just been held up!" yelled the man outside.

"Aye — by the Red Arrow bridge," grunted Scotty, who thought a smart cowboy was trying to be funny. "Git away fr-rom that door before I —"

"I'm not kiddin' yuh, Scotty! This is Dan Shipley. I tell yuh, there's been a holdup."

"Chuck! Wake up, ye sleepin' angel! Don't ye hear the man yellin' bad news? Git up and find Slim, can't ye?"

"What the hell is wrong with yuh, yuh kilt-wearin' bog-trotter?" demanded Chuck Ring sleepily. "Lemme 'lone."

"Where'll I find Slim Caldwell?" asked Shipley anxiously.

"Sweatin' blood at the Red Arrow Saloon," grunted Scotty. "He was seven dollars loser when I left him."

The man went running up the wooden sidewalk and Scotty fell back into his blankets.

"Holdup, eh?" grunted Chuck. "I'll bet they got a million dollars. The Overland carries millions."

"Millions!" snorted Scotty. "There ain't that much."

"Oh, yes, there is. That Overland carries —"

"Where to? Do ye think the millionaires send their money out for a ride? Mebby we better git up, eh?"

"Which way did they go, Scotty?"

"Which way did who go?"

"The robbers."

"How in hell would I know?"

"Yuh hadn't ought to overlook little details like that."

"Ye make me tired, Chuck."

"Ho-o-o-o — hum-m-m-m-m! I hope Slim decides to wait until mornin'. Yuh can't do nothin' in the dark, anyway."

And that was just what Slim Caldwell decided to do. He went to the depot and talked with the train crew and messenger, getting all the details as they had seen them, and then came back.

The train went on, all of an hour off its regular schedule.

Slim didn't have the slightest hope of catching the lone bandit, who had had over half of the night to make his getaway. To the east of the tracks, only a couple of miles away, was the lava country, a land of broken lava where little grew, and where a man might hide away for an indefinite length of time.

The man was alone on the job, which would make it even more difficult than if it had been done by a gang. The description given by the three men might cover half of the men in the valley. There had been nothing conspicuous about the man's actions or apparel. He wore a large black hat, dark shirt, overalls tucked in the tops of his boots.

"Sweet chance to find that whipperwill," sighed Slim. "Half the men in the valley dress thataway, and they all pack guns."

"Look for a man wearin' a black mask," suggested Chuck.

"And carryin' a million dollars," grinned Scotty. "How much did he get, Slim?"

"Nobody knows. The messenger didn't talk much, but the engineer told me that the man was loaded down with stuff — and they don't ship pig-iron nor spuds in that through safe."

"I tell yuh they carry millions in that safe," said Chuck.

"Aw, go to sleep," said Slim. "We hit the grit at daylight, and we'll be a long time on a horse."

CHAPTER
NINE

At the Circle Spade

Chuckwalla Ike was up a little after daylight. He had a headache and a dark-brown taste in his mouth, which caused his long mustaches to assume a forlorn angle. He spilled the hot cake batter on the floor and cut himself in slicing the bacon.

Monty Adams and Steve Winchell had not been to town the night before, for the simple reason that it had not been payday on the Circle Spade, and because they were both broke. They joked with Chuckwalla, who was in no mood to joke, and ate their breakfast.

"Did the old man get drunk?" asked Steve, mopping off his plate with a hunk of bread.

"Not to my knowledge. I lost him early in the game. But I got drunk 'f anybody stops to ask yuh. But I'm all through. Feller's a fool to drink."

"Was anybody playin' the games at the Eagle?" queried Monty.

"Everybody. Rance won — gosh, I dunno how much. Why, him and Angel dealt first ace for five thousand, and Rance won. First card off the deck was an ace. Jim Langley dealt 'em. And I seen Rance win eight one-hundred-dollar bets, hand-runnin', on the black-jack. He busted the game. Fact. And then he set in on the stud game and won thirteen hundred on one hand. Had an ace in the hole and three more in sight, while Angel held a ten-full on queens."

"Holy cats! And did he quit with all that money?"

"I per-sume he did, Monty. If Angel ain't busted, he's sure bent like a pretzel."

"Rance ain't up yet, eh?"

Chuckwalla shook his head slowly.

"I ain't seen hide ner horn of him since he left the Eagle, but I think he's in bed upstairs."

"Well, we shore missed a good evenin'," sighed Steve, shoving away from the table. They went down toward the corral, and Chuckwalla sat down to drink a cup of black coffee. It was about the only thing that appealed to his appetite just now.

He heard a step in the doorway, and turned to see old Rance. The old man was bootless, his hair uncombed, and over his right temple was a bruised lump almost as large as an egg. His eyes were bloodshot, and he seemed unsteady.

"Well, f'r God's sake!" blurted Chuckwalla. "Rance, you're a mess!"

"Yeah," nodded Rance wearily. "Mess."

He came over to the table and sank down in a chair, feeling tenderly of the lump on his head, while Chuckwalla looked him over seriously.

"Somebody must 'a' petted yuh right smart," was his verdict. "I'll heat up some water and see if it won't take some of the swellin' out of the pinnacle."

He bustled back to the stove and filled the kettle.

"I lost yuh last night, Rance. Climbed plumb over my bronc, jist tryin' to get aboard. Mamma, I shore was drunk! A feller of my age ort to be more careful. Did you git here ahead of me?"

"I dunno, Chuckwalla."

"Well, I don't. Who hit yuh, Rance?"

Rance blinked slowly, his eyes focussed on the oilcloth covering of the table.

"I dunno."

"No? You must 'a' been pretty drunk yoreself. I'm goin' to put a little vinegar in this water. They say it's good to pull down a swellin'. Sore, ain't it? Uh-huh. Looks like it might 'a' been caused with a six-gun bar'l. I pistol-whipped a feller once, and he was thataway all over. Figurin' his normal skin as sea-level, I shore gave him altitude."

"That warm water feels good, Chuckwalla."

"You must 'a' got hit hard, Rance."

"Why?"

"You ain't swore once."

"Guess I'm gittin' old."

"We both are — too dam' old to be foolish. I looked for yuh to kill Billy DuMond."

"I didn't. He's a coward, Chuckwalla. I used to be a gun-man. But I'm old now. They don't realize I'm old. Most any man in the valley could beat me to a gun, but they don't know it."

"Do yuh think that's too sore to use horse-liniment on? Mebby it is. Skin's busted. Funny about Lila comin' to warn yuh, Rance."

"Funny?"

"Queer, I meant."

"Queer — yeah."

"Wish you'd saved that letter, Rance."

"Yeah. Don't squeeze that swellin'."

Came the sound of horses walking on the hard-packed ground of the ranch-yard. Chuckwalla stepped to the door and looked outside.

Slim Caldwell, the sheriff, Chuck Ring and Scotty McKay were dismounting near the kitchen door. Chuckwalla turned his head and glanced quickly at Rance, who was holding the wet compress to his temple.

"Got company," said Chuckwalla softly. "Officially."

Old Rance did not look up until the three officers were in the doorway. Slim Caldwell looked curiously at old Rance.

"What have yuh been doin' to yoreself, Rance?" he asked.

"Gittin' bumped," shortly.

"Shore looks like it."

"You fellers must 'a' got up before breakfast," said Chuckwalla, grinning.

"Ye guessed it," nodded McKay, sniffing at the odors of coffee. Chuckwalla knew that was an acceptance of his unvoiced invitation, and he proceeded to add to the pot of coffee and to slice more bacon.

Old Rance wiped his face with a towel, threw the compress into the wash-basin, and leaned back wearily in his chair. The three officers sat down around the table and rolled smokes, while Chuckwalla prepared breakfast.

"Quite a night, wasn't it?" boomed Chuck Ring. "The last I seen of Chuckwalla he was imitatin' a goat with blind-staggers."

"I shore got wobbly," grinned Chuckwalla.

"You didn't drink much, didja, Rance?" queried Caldwell.

Rance shook his head. "I never do, Slim."

"I never did see yuh drunk."

"A man is a fool to git drunk, Slim."

"Aw, yuh don't need to preach," said Chuckwalla quickly, jerking back from the explosive splatter of an egg in hot grease.

"I'm not preachin'," said Rance. "Some folks can't carry their liquor."

"That's me," laughed Chuckwalla. "How do yuh like yore aigs, Slim?"

"Fresh."

"All right, sheriff. But I warn yuh, they're tasteless. Set up ag'in' the table, will yuh? There's milk in the can. Say, I hope some day I'll work on a cow-ranch where they have cow-milk. Been a cowhand all m' life, and all the milk I've ever seen was in cans. And that butter was shipped from Nebrasky. Sometimes we do accidently eat our own beef."

There was plenty of good-natured banter during the breakfast, except from old Rance, who smoked his pipe and shot an occasional quizzical glance at the sheriff. It was unusual for the entire force of officers to be riding together at that time in the morning.

86

They finished their breakfast and shoved back from the table to enjoy their cigarettes. Old Chuckwalla gathered up the dishes and swept the table clean with a wet cloth. He knew something was wrong.

"Where's Monty and Steve?" asked Slim.

"Gone to work," said Chuckwalla.

"They wasn't in town last night, was they?"

"They're broke."

"Good and sufficient reason," grinned Chuck Ring. "Lot more cow-rasslers are broke this mornin'."

Old Rance knocked the dottle out of his pipe, shoved the pipe in his pocket, and leaned forward on the table, facing the sheriff.

"What's wrong, Slim?" he asked abruptly.

"Wrong?" Slim rubbed his nose thoughtfully.

"You three ain't ridin' for yore health."

"We-e-ell, we ain't — exactly, Rance. Last night about midnight the Overland was held up at Curlew Spur. Flagged 'em down with a red lantern, broke the express car and engine loose, ran up to the end of the big cut near the bridge, and blowed the express car safe. One-man job. Knowed how to do it, I reckon. We was down there at daylight, lookin' the place over — and kinda thought we'd drop in for breakfast with yuh."

"Blew the Overland safe, eh?" snorted Chuckwalla. "Well, sir, I've often wondered why somebody —"

Chuckwalla shrugged his shoulders and turned back to the dish-pan.

"One man," said Slim thoughtfully. "It takes nerve to do a job of that kind, Rance."

"How much did they git, Slim?"

"We don't know yet. The messenger says there was a lot of stuff in the safe, but he don't know what it was worth."

"Prob'ly got well paid for a few minutes' work," said Chuck Ring. "That's the way to pull a job — alone."

"Safest way," nodded old Rance. "Split with nobody and keep yore mouth shut."

"What was his description?" asked Chuckwalla.

"Not worth repeatin'," said Slim. "It would cover half of the men in the Valley."

"Nobody got hurt, eh?" questioned old Rance.

"Not that we know about. The messenger got his gun and emptied it, after the robber left the car, and they said the robber fired a shot or two back at him. Just shootin' in the dark."

"It wasn't done by a gr-r-reenhorn," declared Scotty. "That job was done by a man who knew what to do; a man who had plenty of nerve."

"No reward yet, is there?" asked Chuckwalla.

"Too soon," said Slim. "But there will be. I've got a hunch that it was a big haul."

"The Overland carries millions a day," said Chuck seriously.

"Let's be goin'," suggested Scotty, getting to his feet. "Chuck's imagination will get the best of him some day."

"I reckon we might as well drift along," agreed the sheriff. "Much obliged for the breakfast, boys."

"You're always welcome," said old Rance, following them to the doorway, where he watched them mount and ride away.

CHAPTER
TEN

Scotty Gets an Earful of Dirt

The three officers rode back toward Red Arrow, riding knee-to-knee along the dusty road.

"Well, what do yuh think, Slim?" asked Chuck, after a long period of silent riding.

The sheriff shook his head slowly, his eyes fixed on the bobbing ears of his mount.

"Looks bad," he said seriously. "That bump on his head might 'a' been caused by a fall from a horse."

"That's what I thought of, Slim. But, by golly, he's cool. His face didn't show nothin' when yuh told him. I watched him close."

Slim drew up his horse and looked back, his brows drawn together in a thoughtful frown. Then —

"Scotty, you go back to the end of that cut, and camp where yuh can watch things. If old Rance knows his saddle horse is lyin' dead near the end of that cut, still wearin' his saddle, he'll prob'ly try to get it away."

"That's a chance we don't want to take," agreed Scotty. "If he comes, what'll I do, Slim?"

"Stop him, Scotty."

"The proper thing to have done would have been to arrest him on the evidence we've already got," said Chuck.

"Mebby you're right," agreed Slim. "But there's two ways of lookin' at it. If he got one of the millions you talk about, arrestin' him won't get it back. He won't run away and leave his ranch; so we don't need to be in a big hurry."

"That's sense," agreed Scotty. "I'll see yuh later."

He turned his horse and rode back toward the south, while Slim Caldwell and Chuck Ring continued on toward Red Arrow.

Scotty McKay didn't like the idea of spending the day out there, standing guard over the body of a dead horse, but he realized the wisdom of protecting their main exhibit. He had turned back just short of the old wagon bridge across the Red Arrow River and headed back toward Curlew Spur. The going was very rough through the brushy hills, but Scotty was not in any great hurry.

He was about five hundred yards from the end of the big cut, following fairly close to the right-of-way fence, when a bullet droned so close to his ear that he almost fell off his horse. The hills echoed back the rattling report of the rifle, but there was no question in Scotty's mind as to which direction the bullet came from. He slid quickly off his saddle, jerked his rifle from the boot, and ducked low in the tangle of brush. The horse turned and trotted back along the fence, hooked the reins around a snag, and stopped short.

Scotty squatted on his heels and debated thought-fully.

"Not over two hundred yards away," he decided. "Report of gun was plenty audible."

He put his hat on the end of his rifle barrel and lifted it above the brush, jiggling it from side to side. But there was no shooting. He put the hat back on his head, scratched his chin reflectively. Scotty was no reckless fool. He realized that he had everything to lose and nothing to gain by exposing himself.

He considered his next move carefully. To his left was a wide expanse of small, brush-filled ravines where he would be able to find plenty of cover. So much cover, in fact, that he would be unable to see anything himself. To his right was the right-of-way fence, a steep bank — and the railroad track.

To crawl through this fence and slide down the bank would be a simple matter. And once in the wide open space of the railroad cut it would also be a simple matter for the other man to fill him full of lead. But, reasoned Scotty, the other man might think the same thing, and not expect him to take such a big chance.

He crawled under the lower wire and out to the edge of the cut, where he leaned out as far as he dared, scanning the bank along the tracks. As far as he could see there was no one in sight. After a minute of deliberation he turned around and lowered his legs over the steep bank.

Slowly he let himself down, gripping the top of the bank with his elbows. He was almost stretched out full length down that bank, working his knees into the soft dirt, getting all ready to let loose and slide to the bottom, when —

Whap!

A bullet thudded into the dirt just under his right hip.

Splug!

Another ripped into the dirt, higher up, and filled his right ear with a spray of gravel. Scotty was stretched out so completely that he was unable to act quickly for a moment, but when he did get going he rolled clear under the right-of-way fence, tearing a great rip across the back of his shirt.

"Whew!"

He sat up and shook the dirt out of his ear, before reaching back to get his rifle. His nose was beaded with perspiration, and the hand that reached for his cigarette-papers trembled exceedingly.

"For a moment I was what an insurance agent would call a bad r-risk," he muttered aloud. "What a fool a man may be! And still, all I got was a dir-r-rty ear and the scare of me young life."

He laid the rifle across his lap, lighted his cigarette and inhaled deeply.

"If ye want me," he grinned softly, "ye know where I am."

For the better part of fifteen minutes Scotty McKay remained motionless. He heard a locomotive whistling for Curlew Spur, and in a few minutes a freight train came along, creaking and groaning, the single engine working hard to pull the long train up the grade. Scotty pinched out the light of his second cigarette, stretched his arms, picked up his rifle and sneaked down through the brush.

Inaction had palled upon him, and he was going to try to find out who had been shooting at him. Slowly he moved ahead, most of the time on his hands and knees. It took him at least thirty minutes to cover a hundred yards, where he came out on the top of a little knoll, heaped high with boulders.

From this vantage-point he could get a good view of the surrounding country. As far as he could see, everything was serene. Farther ahead and to the right was an open swale with the railroad fence across the upper end of it. On the other side of that fence was the end of the big cut, and just beyond the swale, in a clump of brush, was Rance McCoy's saddle horse, dead. A bullet had smashed through its head.

Scotty could not see the horse, but he knew where it was, and he was in a position to see if any one came to molest it. He squinted at the sun, estimated that it would be some time before Slim or Chuck would come to relieve him, made himself as comfortable as possible and prepared to watch.

Slim Caldwell and Chuck Ring went straight back to Red Arrow and dismounted at the depot, where the telegraph operator handed Slim a telegram, which read:

MOVE CAREFULLY FIVE THOUSAND REWARD FOR RETURN OF STOLEN PACKAGES SENDING OPERA-TIVE AND DETAILS

WELLS FARGO

93

"Didn't I tell yuh?" said Chuck. "I said all along that we ought to go careful. They want them packages back. Betcha anythin' yuh want to bet, they got away with a million."

"With all yore hindsight, it's a wonder to me that you never amounted to somethin'," growled Slim. "They never got any million dollars, but they did get enough for the express company to advise movin' carefully."

They mounted their horses and rode back to the court-house, where Slim had a conference with Albert Merkle, the prosecuting attorney. Merkle was as round as a barrel, with a face like a full moon, serving his first term as county prosecutor and taking his position very seriously.

Merkle read the telegram, listened closely to what Slim had to tell him, and then propounded wisely:

"That evidence won't last long unless we take steps to protect it, Slim. A couple of nights, and the coyotes will ruin it for our use."

"Well, we can't file it away in my office," protested Slim.

"No, that's true. I'll go out with you and look at it."

They secured a horse for Merkle at the livery stable, and headed back toward the scene of the robbery. Merkle wanted to have Rance McCoy arrested at once, but Slim demurred.

"Wait'll we find out what he got, Al. It was a one-man job, and if he got a big haul, he's got it planted. He'll never confess, and he'll never tell where the stuff is hid."

"My end of the affair is only interested in a conviction, Slim."

"Yore end of the affair is only interested in justice," corrected Chuck Ring. "Don't be so civilized, Al."

"I guess that's right," laughed Merkle. "It's easy to overlook that angle of it."

They made no attempt at concealment, but rode in at the lower end of the swale. Scotty saw them and stood up among the rocks, calling to them; after which he clawed his way through the brush to the clearing.

"Where's yore horse?" asked Slim.

"Aw, he's back along the railroad fence. Anyway, that's where he was the last time I seen him."

As rapidly as possible Scotty told them what had happened to him.

"Were they trying to kill you, McKay?" asked Merkle.

"Well, I dunno what was on their mind at the time," said Scotty seriously. "It had all the earmarks of intent to kill, Mer-r-rkle."

"And yuh didn't see anybody, eh?" queried Slim anxiously.

"I did not. Ye missed the sight of your life. I tell ye, I was hangin' by my elbows, without any foothold whatever, and I upended myself over the bank and under that wire so fast that I surprised myself. Look at the back of me shirt, will yuh?"

Slim scratched his chin reflectively and scanned the surrounding country, while Merkle shifted uneasily in his saddle.

"We might as well look at the evidence," said Slim.

"Yes; let's get it over with," agreed Merkle heartily.

They rode up to the fence, accompanied by Scotty on foot, and tied their horses. Slim led the way over to where the horse was stretched out in the low brush.

"F'r the love of gosh!" exploded Slim. "Look at that!"

The saddle was missing, and from the upturned rump, which had been graced with the Circle Spade brand, had been skinned a spot about twelve inches square. On the shoulder was another skinned patch, one ear had been cut off close to the head, and the left front leg had been skinned from knee to fetlock.

"And the shoes have been yanked off!" snorted Scotty. "I remember that the animal was shod."

"And there goes yore old evidence," said Chuck dolefully.

Slim whistled unmusically between his teeth.

"They kept me away while they destroyed evidence," said Scotty.

"That was the idea," admitted Slim sadly. He twisted his neck and looked toward the Circle Spade ranch.

"But even at that, you three men saw the animal," said the prosecutor. "You can swear it was a Circle Spade horse; the riding horse of Rance McCoy."

"Sure," nodded Slim quickly. "We saw it, Al. And not only that, but we recognized the old man's saddle."

"What kind of a saddle was it?"

Slim looked quickly at Chuck, who scratched his nose and looked at Scotty.

"I can't tell yuh," said Scotty. "I seen it, too."

"Pshaw!" snorted Slim. "We all seen it, Al; but there ain't a damned one of us that can describe it. I could pick it out, but I can't describe it."

"Not such good evidence," admitted the attorney. "Maybe we better go back to town."

"Yea-a-ah," drawled Slim. "Go get yore bronc, Scotty."

CHAPTER ELEVEN

A Horse Trade

It was early morning in the town of Welcome; the cold gray dawn of a fall morning, with a brisk breeze, which caused the livery-stable keeper to slap his hands violently against his thigh, as he watered a team of horses at the trough in front of the stable.

On the rough porch of a saloon a swamper swept away an accumulation of playing-cards, cigarette-butts, and other litter of a gambling-house and saloon. The cards slithered away in the breeze like autumn leaves. From a blacksmith shop came the musical clank of a hammer on anvil, as the smithy tuned up for his morning task.

Two cowboys came from the doorway of a small hotel, pausing for a moment on the edge of the sidewalk, before crossing the street toward a café. They walked with the peculiar rolling gait of men who wear high-heeled boots, their elbows held closely to their sides, as is the habit of men who spend most of their lives in the saddle.

One cowboy was well over six feet tall, thin, angular. His features were heavily lined, nose rather large, wide mouth, and gray eyes. The other cowboy was less than six feet tall, broad of shoulder, with a square face, out of which beamed a pair of blue eyes, now slightly clouded with sleep. His face was grin-wrinkled and his eyes were nested in a mass of tiny lines, caused from their owner's propensity for seeing the funny side of life.

The tall one was "Hashknife" Hartley, and the other was "Sleepy" Stevens, strangers to Welcome town.

"The wind she blow, pretty soon we have snow, and what will poor robin do then, poor thing?" grinned Sleepy.

"Yu-u-uh betcha!" grunted Hashknife. "She's gettin' a long ways north for summer clothes."

They entered the restaurant and sat down. Just behind them came Bill Warren, former dealer for Angel McCoy at Red Arrow. Warren nodded to them and sat down at their table.

"Been dealin' all night," he said briskly. "Some fellers never know when to quit playin'. Strangers here, ain't yuh?"

"Came in late last night," said Hashknife.

"Goin' to stay?"

"Prob'ly not."

They ceased the conversation long enough to order their breakfast.

"Do they play pretty heavy around here?" asked Sleepy.

"Well, pretty good. Welcome ain't as good as Red Arrow, but we get a pretty fair play here. I've only been here a few days. I'm from Red Arrow. That's northwest of here, less than twenty miles. Pretty good place."

"Good play up there, eh?"

"You bet. Say, you boys don't happen to be lookin' for an investment, do yuh?"

"All depends," said Hashknife seriously.

"I see. Well, what made me ask was the fact that there's a bargain in Red Arrow. Feller by the name of McCoy has kinda broke his pick up there. Owns the Eagle Saloon and gamblin'-house. Pulled a funny deal on his own father, and aced him out of a lot of money. Queered his own game. Fact. I hear he's had to close the place. And he sure had a big play."

"Would he sell cheap?" asked Hashknife, attacking his ham and eggs.

"I'll bet he would. Somewhat of a fool, this McCoy. His father is a tough old gun-man, and they never got along. Oh, it's a salty place up there. Some lone wolf held up the train the other night and got away with a fortune."

"They did, eh?"

Hashknife paused and stared at Warren. Sleepy snorted softly, gazing disconsolately at his platter of food.

"Yuh bet they did," said Warren. "One man pulled it all alone. Broke the train at Curlew Spur, took the engine and express car up the track a ways and blew the safe. I don't know how much he got, but they say he got plenty."

"Prob'ly," nodded Hashknife, stirring his coffee with the handle of his knife.

"And they won't catch him," declared Warren. "Too many places to hide — and one man don't talk, except to himself."

100

"Prob'ly not," said Hashknife absently.

"But that Eagle Saloon would be a mint if it was run right. Angel McCoy is all through. The fixtures are all first-class, and I could help yuh — yuh know what I mean. I know most everybody up there.

"Me and Angel always got along good. He had to turn me loose, because business was pretty bad. Not that I care a damn about Angel. He's salty. His old man ain't very well liked either. Got a bad reputation. Him and Angel never got along, And there's a girl — sister of Angel's. Name's Lila. She just got back from school, I understand. She's about twenty years old. I ain't never met the lady, but I can say she's a mighty pretty girl. I heard a rumor that she wasn't Angel's sister, and that she just found out that old Rance ain't her father. Anyway, she had quit the ranch and was livin' in town when I left there. They say Angel is stuck on her, but she'd be a fool to marry him. He's crooked; and it don't pay to play crooked in that town. Them cattlemen sabe poker, and they sure declare an open season on yuh the first time yuh make a break."

"Pretty near time for the fall roundup, ain't it?" asked Hashknife.

"Sure. If you go up there, look into that proposition. I'll bet you could buy Angel out for a song. He's all through in that country."

They finished their breakfast and walked out to the main street of Welcome.

"Well, we might as well start, I suppose," said Sleepy dolefully.

"Start where?"

"Don't try to be funny, Hashknife. Yore neck stretched a foot when he mentioned that holdup."

"Oh, yeah."

"Oh, yeah," mimicked Sleepy. "Now, don't tell me you're interested in their fall roundup."

"With twenty dollars between us — I ought to."

"And you talkin' about investin' in a saloon."

"I didn't. He asked me if we was lookin' over the place, and I intimated we was interested enough to invest what we had in a payin' proposition. He didn't need to know we had only twenty dollars, did he? And yuh learn a lot more about conditions if they think you've got money."

"That may be true, but just the same I don't know of any good reason why we should go to Red Arrow. It's only a little range, Hashknife. It won't be long before the old snow will be cuttin' across this country, and it'll shore catch two unworthy punchers with thin seats in their pants, if them two punchers don't do somethin'. We started out for Arizona, if yuh remember. It's summer down there, cowboy. I want to read about my snow this winter. And as far as that train robbery is concerned — nobody got hurt."

Hashknife leaned against a post and rolled a cigarette, a half-smile on his thin lips, as he glanced at the serious face of Sleepy Stevens.

"Sleepy, I'm goin' to foller you this time. You've always trailed my bets, and for once in our lives I'm goin' to foller you. Head for Arizona, cowboy; and I'll rub knees with yuh. C'mon."

"My God!" exclaimed Sleepy. "I'll betcha you're sick. Don'tcha feel kinda faint? Any spots in front of yore eyes? Kinda ache all over? No?"

"I feel normal," grinned Hashknife.

"Yuh shore don't act it. Huh! Well, mebby I'm dreamin'. After while I'll wake up and find myself bein' shot at by somebody you're trailin'. Let's go, before yuh suffer a relapse."

They went down to the livery stable, where an unkempt, sleepy-eyed stable-man met them. He squinted at Hashknife, spat violently, and glanced back along the row of stalls.

"We're pullin' out," said Hashknife. "What's our bill?"

"Oh, about fo' bits. Say" — he squinted at Hashknife — "one of you fellers was a-ridin' a tall, gray bronc, wasn't yuh?"

"I ride him," said Hashknife.

"Uh-huh. Well, I shore wondered about it. Seemed to me I remembered yuh did, but I wasn't sure. I don't like to say too much, but I'm plumb scared that somebody got color-blind early this mornin'."

"What do yuh mean?" asked Hashknife quickly.

"C'mere and take a look."

He led them farther down the stable, halting behind Sleepy's sorrel gelding. On the left was an empty stall and on the right stood a rough-looking, dark bay horse, with one cropped ear and a hammer-head. It turned and looked at the men, an evil glint in its eyes.

"That's where yore gray stood," declared the stable-man. "I put yore broncs together. Early this mornin' I heard somebody ride in and put up a horse. I didn't git up. Folks usually take care of their own bronc at that time in the mornin'. But when I got up I didn't find no extra horse in here, and when I went to feed 'em, I shore noticed that yore horse has turned color quite a bit."

"That's not my horse," said Hashknife.

"Shore it ain't. And it's lame, too. Picked up a stone. I dug it out a while ago and filled the place with some axle-grease."

"What's the brand on it?"

"Half-Box R."

"Who owns that brand?"

"Feller by the name of Reimer — Butch Reimer. His ranch is about eight miles from here, between here and Red Arrer. Yuh can't tell who owns the horse now, of course."

"He'd probably know who owns it," said Sleepy.

"Prob'ly might."

"What kind of a feller?" asked Hashknife.

"Plumb forked, Butch is, and he hires a forked crew. Honest, as far as I know, though. That ain't such a bad animal, at that. Betcha he'd stand a lot."

"Betcha he'd give a lot, too," smiled Hashknife. "Is he too lame to travel?"

"Might be. Be all right t'morrow."

Hashknife and Sleepy went outside, sat down on the sidewalk and considered the situation. While Hashknife voiced no complaint, Sleepy knew that the tall cowboy would go through fire to get that gray horse back again.

"We'll wait until that bronc is able to travel, Sleepy. One more day won't make nor break us."

"You mean to say you'd pull out and leave some danged thief to own Ghost?"

"Well, it — it can't be helped, Sleepy. It would take a long time to hunt down a horse-thief in this country. We'll rest up until to-morrow and then head for Arizona."

"We will like hell! We'll head for the Half-Box R ranch and find out who owns that crow-bait."

Hashknife smiled thoughtfully at Sleepy. "You ain't just tryin' to play the game back at me, are yuh?"

"Not a bit."

"Well, I'm really glad, Sleepy. It's time we quit foolin' around. We're gettin' old, me and you; kinda mellow. Why, a few years ago, I'd 'a' started out after that horse-thief on foot. But I'm slowin' up, I tell yuh."

"Yea-a-ah, I'll betcha. You'll prob'ly kiss him when we find him. Trade yore gun for a cane, grandpa. Let's go and get us a drink."

Welcome was a smaller town than Red Arrow, and it did not take the stable-man long to spread the news that somebody had stolen a horse from one of the strange cowboys.

A number of people went down to look at the Half-Box R horse, but none of them seemed to be able to tell who owned it. Butch Reimer was well known in Welcome, and as far as Hashknife was able to find out, he bore a fairly good reputation as a cattleman.

The thief had been thoughtful enough to take his own saddle, which was something for Hashknife to be thankful for, as his saddle had been made to order. There was no further news of the robbery, although they heard several people discussing it during the day.

They spent the day playing pool, which was a favorite diversion with both of them. During one of the games Sleepy grew thoughtful, which was unusual with him.

"I was thinkin' about that big robbery," he said, when they were in their room that night. "They ought to pay a good reward for the return of that much money."

Hashknife's indifference nettled Sleepy.

"Oh, . . . all right!" he snorted. "For once in our misguided lives, let's show a little sense."

"I'm with yuh — if I never see the back of my neck."

"Then you're a changed man," declared Sleepy.

"Gettin' old, I reckon."

Hashknife stretched wearily, but his thin lips were smiling as he stripped off his thin, much-washed blue shirt, disclosing a lean, muscular torso. He had long arms, big hands; and his muscles rippled under his bronzed skin, as he snapped his arms back and forth in short arm punches which would have floored a man.

His waist was narrow, hips long and lean, and with his high-heeled boots off he moved with the grace of a cat.

Sleepy watched him admiringly.

"Too bad yuh didn't take up prize-fightin', Hashknife."

"Yeah, I suppose," smiled Hashknife. "How about you?"

"I don't think fast enough."

"And I'd probably sit down to think, durin' a fight."

"I'll bet yuh would. If somebody mentioned a mystery, it's a cinch you'd forget what yuh was doin', Hashknife."

"It's a failin', I suppose. Ho-o-o-hum! We better hit the hay if we're startin' early."

And Sleepy knew that it was not a job at the roundup that was calling Hashknife. The moment the gambler had mentioned the train robbery Sleepy knew what would happen. He had been Hashknife's partner long enough to know the inner workings of that long cowboy's mind, and he knew the mention of that holdup to Hashknife was like a spur to a broncho.

It meant a chance to pit his mind against crime and criminals; not so much because he disliked criminals, but because of the dangerous game.

Hashknife had never studied psychology, nor had he ever tried to analyze crime. Born of poor parents — his father had been an itinerant minister in the Milk River country, in Montana — he had had little schooling. At an early age he had started out to make his own way in the world, working as a cowboy, the only profession he knew.

But he had a receptive mind, and in the years that followed he had picked up a varied education, absorbing the things that are often overlooked by other men, more fortunate in their earlier years; studying human nature, but always analyzing things. He wanted to know the why of everything.

Drifting one day to the ranch, the brand of which gave him his nickname, he met Dave Stevens, another wandering cowboy, who became "Sleepy" because he seemed always wide awake, and these two mounted their horses one day, strapped on their war-bags and bed-rolls, and started out to see the other side of the hill.

And since that day they had seen many ranges and the other side of many hills; but there were always more ranges ahead — more hills to cross. It had not been a profitable partnership as far as money was concerned. Right now they had less money than they had the day they left the old Hashknife ranch; but behind them were memories that money could not buy; memories of people who prayed that some day these two cowboys might come back and help enjoy the happiness their work had wrought.

Life had made them fatalists. Death had struck at them many times, but missed. Sometimes it was very close. They both bore scars of conflict, and they fully realized the danger of their work; realized that some day the pendulum of fortune might swing the wrong way.

In many localities they were marked men. Their reputation was well known, and among those who worked outside the law, they were spoken of as something to be avoided. Neither of them was a split-second gun-man, nor were they of the dead-shot variety; but many times had they walked out of a powder-smoke haze unscathed, while gun-men had to be carried out feet-first.

CHAPTER
TWELVE

The Half-Box R

"A hundred and thirty-two thousand dollars!" exploded Chuck Ring. "Didn't I tell yuh, Slim? Didn't I? By golly, I knew what I was talkin' about, didn't I?"

"You said a million," reminded Scotty McKay.

"What's the difference? Dang near a million, ain't it? I'll betcha you wouldn't know the difference, if yuh saw the two amounts together. Just think of a hundred and thirty-two thousand! Why, yuh can't ee-magine it!"

"Takes brains," admitted Scotty seriously.

The representative of the express company nodded gravely, sucking heavily on his cigar. He was seated in the sheriff's office, occupying the extra chair, while the two deputies squatted against the wall. Slim Caldwell leaned back in his chair, feet crossed on top of his desk, a frown between his eyes.

"That's what it amounts to," said the Wells Fargo man. "There's a five-thousand-dollar reward."

"And who in hell," said Chuck querulously, "would be fool enough to trade yuh a hundred and thirty-two thousand dollars for five thousand?"

"That all depends on the point of view."

"Well, I know what mine would be."

"Yuh spoke of valuable packages," said Slim.

"Yes, I did. There are two packages, each containing fifty cut diamonds. These packages are worth twenty-five thousand each. There is one small package containing a single diamond ring, worth ten thousand dollars. Another package contains five platinum and diamond watches, valued at seven thousand. A package of currency worth thirty-five thousand, a canvas sack of gold worth ten thousand, and a package of negotiable bonds, worth twenty thousand. In all there were seven packages."

"Good God!" snorted Chuck. "Some fellers shore do have all the luck. If I held up that train, I'd prob'ly get a mail-order catalogue."

"You say you are not a detective," said Slim.

"I am not; I merely represent the company. I don't know what good a detective would do in a case of this kind. It is merely a case of a lone bandit holding up the train and making his getaway. His capture would consist more of luck than anything else. As you have said, the description of the robber would fit half the men in the Valley. And as far as that is concerned, any one man in the Valley could have done the job."

"And he'd be a sucker to give it back," declared Chuck.

"We don't expect him to give it back. But to the man who can recover that money — or rather the packages, intact — we will give five thousand dollars."

Slim did not tell the Wells Fargo man about his suspicions in regard to Rance McCoy, but Merkle, the prosecutor, did, and the man came straight back to Slim about it.

"With all that evidence, why don't you arrest him, sheriff?"

"I can," said Slim. "But you'll never get yore stuff back. Old Rance McCoy would see you and yore company in hell before he'd squawk. If you want to pay a hundred and thirty-two thousand dollars for puttin' him in jail — it's yore money. And if Merkle don't quit blattin' about what he knows, we'll never get it."

"The prosecutor wants a conviction, of course."

"And you want the money back," said Slim dryly. "Mebby you better tell Merkle to keep his mouth shut, eh?"

"Might be a good idea, sheriff."

"Best in the world."

Slim Caldwell left Chuck and Scotty at the office, saddled his horse and rode away. He thought of going down to the Circle Spade and having a heart-to-heart talk with old Rance, and was almost to the ranch before he decided to postpone it for a while.

And instead of going to see old Rance, he swung off to the right and went down to the big cut along the railroad. The coyotes and magpies had been busy at the carcass of their Exhibit A, and there was little left of it. Below the big cut, near Curlew Spur, was a crossing, where Slim crossed the tracks and headed for the Half-Box R. It was not over two miles to Butch Reimer's ranch, and Slim found Butch at home with Billy DuMond. The rest of the crew were working.

Butch greeted the sheriff pleasantly enough, but his small eyes showed a certain curiosity over the sheriff's visit. DuMond had not been to Red Arrow since Rance

McCoy had practically run him out of town, and Slim thought he acted a trifle sheepish about it, although nothing was said about the incident.

"What's new on the robbery?" asked Butch.

"Nothin' much, Butch. He got a hundred and thirty-two thousand dollars' worth."

"What do yuh know about that! Gosh, that was worth goin' after, Slim."

"Shore was."

"Who have we here?" grunted DuMond.

Hashknife and Sleepy were riding up through the big gate, heading directly to the ranch-house.

"I never seen them two before," said DuMond.

"Howdy," greeted Butch, getting to his feet.

The two cowboys dismounted and led their horses up to the porch.

"Howdy, folks," smiled Hashknife. "Is this the Half-Box R outfit?"

"This is her," nodded Butch.

"Fine. Take a look at that bay and see if yuh can remember who owned it last."

Butch walked down the steps and looked the animal over. Slim also moved down and examined the animal.

"Wears my brand," said Butch thoughtfully. "I don't just remember that particular animal. What about him, stranger?"

"That particular animal," said Hashknife slowly, "was left in place of my horse, night before last, in Welcome."

"Yea-a-ah? Well, I'll be darned!"

112

"And I thought yuh might know who owned the animal."

"No-o-o-o, I can't say I do. Funny he'd leave this horse and take yore animal."

"This one had a sore foot. That's why we're a day late in lookin' up that light-fingered jigger's family tree."

Butch Reimer laughed softly and looked at Hashknife. Slim did not grin. He studied the horse closely and turned to Hashknife.

"I'm the sheriff of this county," he said. "Name's Slim Caldwell."

Hashknife thrust out his hand quickly.

"Pleased to meet yuh, sheriff. My name's Hartley. Meet my pardner, Stevens."

Slim introduced them to Reimer and DuMond.

"Goin' to be around here a while, Hartley?" asked Butch.

"Long enough to see who got my bronc."

"Oh, yeah. If you're lookin' for work, there'll be plenty of it. Roundup starts in a week or so, and there ain't too many cow-hands in this country."

"We're headin' for Arizona," explained Hashknife.

"Goin' down where it's hot, eh?"

"Why don't yuh jist keep that horse?" queried DuMond. "He's as good as you'll find."

"Not if I can find mine," smiled Hashknife.

"Lost horses are always best," laughed DuMond.

"It ain't so much the difference in the animals," said Hashknife. "I like to keep what I own."

"Well, I never quarreled much if I got a fair exchange."

"*You* probably wouldn't."

DuMond took a good look at Hashknife's gray eyes and decided not to carry the conversation any further.

"You boys goin' on to Red Arrow?" asked Slim.

"We didn't intend to," replied Hashknife. "I'm sorry yuh don't remember who owned that horse, 'cause I'd shore like to find the ex-owner and explain the difference between this bronc and the one he took from me."

"Might as well take a look at the town," suggested Sleepy. "We're this far, so we might as well go on."

"Sure," agreed Slim heartily. "Ride along with me."

They left the Half-Box R and rode away toward Red Arrow together. Slim was not very communicative, and Hashknife noticed that he looked often at the bay horse.

"Not wishin' to get personal on short acquaintance," smiled Hashknife, "but haven't you an idea who owned this horse, sheriff?"

"I can't swear that I do, Hartley. Yuh might be fooled in a bay horse, so I better keep my mouth shut. Stealin' horses is a crime in this country, yuh know."

"I thought it might be. It is in several places I've been. Down at Welcome I was talkin' to a gambler, who used to deal at the Eagle in Red Arrow, and he told me quite a lot about the place. His name was Warren."

"Oh, yeah; Bill Warren. I heard he was down there. The Eagle has closed its doors."

"He said it probably would. Did McCoy go busted?"

114

"More than likely. His old man won pretty close to eight thousand the night before it closed."

"Did he pay it?"

Slim laughed shortly. "I dunno. Don't see how he could. That's a lot of money, Hartley. Remember that feller DuMond yuh just met at the ranch? Well, old Rance McCoy danged near killed him that night. He shore made DuMond crawl."

"Rance McCoy is pretty salty, eh?"

"About ninety-nine per cent."

They crossed the river and were almost to town when Slim Caldwell looked sharply at Hashknife.

"You don't happen to be any relation to a feller named Hartley that was up on the Thunder River range for a while a year or so ago, do yuh?"

"I dunno," replied Hashknife. "There's more or less Hartleys scattered over the country."

"Not this kind of a Hartley."

"Colored one?" grinned Hashknife.

"Pretty much white, as far as I've heard."

"I guess it wasn't any of my relatives, sheriff."

"Prob'ly not. It just struck me kinda queer that there should be two Hartleys runnin' around with Stevens for a bunkie."

Hashknife's face did not change expression, and when the sheriff looked at Sleepy, there was only mild wonder in that worthy's innocent blue eyes.

"That shore *is* funny," said Sleepy seriously.

"There's a lot of queer things in the world," said Hashknife. "It kinda amazes us three to think that there should be two sets of Hartleys and Stevens runnin' loose thataway. In fact, there ain't many folks that would believe it; so let's not tell anybody else, sheriff."

Slim eased himself in his saddle and nodded shortly.

"I don't want to make myself out a liar," he said seriously. "As far as I know, there's only one set."

"And that's no lie," smiled Hashknife.

They rode past the little schoolhouse and saw Lila and Angel on the porch, talking to each other. Hashknife happened to see the expression on Slim's face when he saw Lila and Angel, and he knew the sheriff was annoyed.

"That was Angel McCoy and Lila Stevens," said Slim. "At least, they say her name is Stevens."

"Thasso?" grunted Sleepy. "What do yuh know about that? I've knowed a lot of folks named Stevens, but she's the first one I ever felt like scrapin' up relationship with."

CHAPTER
THIRTEEN

Two Suspects

Lila had sent for Angel. After what had happened in the Eagle that night, she felt that she would never want to speak to him again; but she wanted to know what was in that letter. Angel had only blurted a few words.

But he refused to tell her any more. He seemed to blame her for all his hard luck, which was manifestly unfair.

"Why didn't you keep out of there?" he asked her. "You ruined everything. Even if Rance McCoy *had* practically busted my bank — he had brought the crowd back to my place, and I'd get it all back with interest. But if you want to know so much about yourself, I'll tell yuh this much: your mother died in an insane asylum, and your father was shot for robbing a bank."

Lila stepped back against the building, her face growing white, her eyes widening in horror.

"Angel, that is not true!" she gasped. "You are lying, just to hurt me."

He shook his head quickly.

"No, I'm not lyin'. I tell yuh, it's true. Rance McCoy can't deny it. I had it all in writin' — but he tore it up.

117

Oh, I can get another letter. Or you might write to the sheriff of Medicine Tree. He dug up the information for me."

Angel turned and walked away, leaving her staring after him, her eyes full of misery. Her mother insane! Her father a thief! What a parentage!

She dismissed school for the afternoon, and the fifteen pupils went whooping away across the school yard. As she walked back down the street toward Parker's home, it seemed as though every one on the street was looking at her, talking about her.

Suddenly she looked up. In front of her stood Rance McCoy. He was looking at her seriously, his mouth twisted a little, as though he wanted to smile, but was afraid.

For several moments they looked at each other. Then —

"Yuh look like you'd jist seen a ghost, Lila," he said.

Ghost! She wondered if he had talked with Angel.

"You ain't sick, are yuh, Lila?"

"Sick?" Her voice sounded hoarse. "I — I guess I am. I talked with Angel to-day."

Old Rance peered closely at her, coming nearer.

"You talked with Angel, eh? What about, Lila?"

"About my — my parents."

"Yea-a-ah?" The old man's lips tightened and he rubbed the knuckles of his right hand along the filled loops of his cartridge-belt.

"He's bitter," she said, as though defending him.

"Bitter, is he?" Rance laughed harshly. "Oh, I suppose he is — the dirty sidewinder."

"He's your son, Rance McCoy."

"That don't stop him from bein' a sidewinder, does it?"

"Perhaps not. Oh, I'm sorry I went to the Eagle that night. I suppose it was none of my business, but he had admitted to me that he dealt crooked with you. You had already given him so much, you know."

"I'm glad yuh came," he said slowly. "It kinda showed that yuh — yuh hadn't forgotten the old man. Angel hates me. He's always hated me, Lila. And I'm gettin' so old that it hurts to be hated."

"I'm sorry. I — I don't hate you. But it wasn't fair to never let me know who I was. Angel swears that I came to expose him that night in order to — to get some of your money."

"Some of *my* money, eh?" Old Rance smiled bitterly.

"He brags about how much of it he got."

"Does he? It's worth braggin' about, Lila. How is yore school comin' along?"

"All right. I love the work."

"Well, that's fine. It's good honest work, Lila. We miss yuh out at the Circle Spade — me and Chuckwalla."

"I may come out some day," she said.

"That would sure be fine, Lila."

He watched her go on down the street, and then went over to the Red Arrow bank, where he found Merkle, the prosecuting attorney, talking with the cashier. Merkle and Rance had never been friends; so they ignored each other.

Down at the Sheriff's office Chuck Ring was making a close examination of the horse Hashknife had ridden, and when he went back into the office he declared he knew the owner of the horse.

"That's the horse Kid Glover's been ridin'," he stated. "He broke the animal himself. There's a scar on its left shoulder where it bulked into a hitchin'-post over by the Red Arrow Saloon. If Butch Reimer says he don't know that horse, he's either mistaken or lyin' about it."

"Are yuh sure of it, Chuck?" asked Slim.

"Jist as sure as hell. You go look at it, Scotty."

Scotty McKay grinned and shook his head.

"Don't need to," he said. "I knew the animal the moment I seen it; but I didn't know whether it was supposed to be recognized or not."

"And what kind of a jigger is Kid Glover?" asked Hashknife.

"If Kid Glover was in town, and yuh heard a dog yelp, you'd know who kicked it," said Chuck Ring.

Hashknife grinned at Chuck.

"That's sure givin' him a bad name, Ring."

"He's a bad boy," said Slim seriously. "Arizona puncher, ignorant as hell. He's kept pretty well out of trouble around here, but he's got the earmarks of a bad actor."

"Well, we might as well go back there and teach him the difference between bay and gray," said Sleepy.

"Sheriff, do yuh suppose he's ignorant enough to make that trade in Welcome and come back to the ranch with the gray horse?" asked Hashknife.

Slim shook his head quickly.

"The Kid is ignorant, but that don't mean he's a fool. You'll have to look further than the Half-Box R, Hartley."

"That's what I was thinkin'."

"But why would Butch Reimer deny knowin' the horse?" wondered Scotty McKay.

"Now, you're talkin'," grunted Chuck.

"And that's about all," said Slim quickly. "Butch Reimer ain't so poor he has to steal horses."

"Well, it looks to me as though I better be satisfied with the trade," grinned Hashknife. "I dunno just where we're goin', but when we get there I'll drop yuh a card. That gray horse will weight close to twelve hundred, and on his left shoulder is a Cross-in-a-Box brand. He's five years old and he'll buck when the spirit moves him."

"I'll shore keep an eye out for him, Hartley," said Slim. "If he shows up, I'll get him for yuh."

"Thanks."

Hashknife and Sleepy walked outside to their horses, followed by the sheriff and his men. Hashknife mounted, but Sleepy merely untied his animal, looking curiously at Hashknife.

"Do yuh mean that we're headin' back?" asked Sleepy.

"Sure," said Hashknife seriously. "We'll sleep in Welcome to-night, and then head south in the mornin'."

"We will!" blurted Sleepy. "What's the matter with you — losin' yore grip, cowboy? Do you mean to set there and tell me that you're goin' to let an ignorant puncher forcibly trade yuh out of Ghost?"

"Well, it might take a long time, Sleepy. You wanted to go to Arizona pretty bad, and I just thought —"

"Well, we ain't goin' — jist yet. Arizona won't move away, will it? Git off that bronc and let's find a place to sleep."

"We-e-e-ell, all right," grudgingly. "I suppose I've got to go through life humorin' yuh, feller. I hope some day to have my own way in somethin'."

But Sleepy knew Hashknife's true feelings in the matter; knew that it would break Hashknife's heart to go away and leave Ghost in the hands of some one else. And he knew that the puzzle of the train robbery was calling Hashknife to action.

With all Sleepy's objections to working with Hashknife in solving these range mysteries, he was just as eager to mix into them as was Hashknife.

Scotty McKay went with them to the livery stable and to the hotel. When they went back to the office they found Slim talking with Merkle. After Merkle went away Slim called Hashknife aside.

"You heard some of the talk about old Rance McCoy beatin' the Eagle games out of close to eight thousand, didn't yuh?" asked Slim.

Hashknife said he had.

"Well," continued Slim, "here's the queer part of it. The old man drew seventy-five hundred from the bank that day — every cent he had. Now, he won close to eight thousand, which would make his roll close to sixteen thousand dollars. To-day, so Merkle tells me, the old man borrowed five hundred from the bank."

"And you think the old man robbed that train, eh?"

"Who told yuh that?"

"Nobody; I just felt it."

"Uh-huh; and I'll tell yuh why, Hartley."

Slim explained about finding Rance McCoy's horse near the spot where the safe had been blown, and some of the things that happened during the actual blowing of the safe. He told Hashknife about the bruise on the old man's head, and of the shots that had been fired at Scotty, when he went back to guard their evidence.

"Maybe somebody stole the horse," said Hashknife.

"If they did, why didn't the old man say something about it? He's never said a word about it. And the men who shot at Scotty took away the saddle, after skinnin' off all the brands and identifyin' marks."

"How does it happen that yuh never arrested him?"

"Stole too much money. Amounts to over a hundred thousand, and when a man steals that much it's pretty hard to put him in jail until after the money is found, yuh know."

"That's all right; but how are yuh goin' to find out?"

"And there yuh are," sighed Slim.

"You spoke about Angel McCoy goin' broke. The robbery was a one-man job."

"That's true. I tell yuh, Hartley, there's a lot of men in this county that would probably take a chance on that much money."

"Yuh don't need to confine yourself to *this* county."

123

"I suppose not. I'm no detective. I believe one third of what I hear, and a half of all I see. I'm no closer to findin' out who robbed that train than I was the night it happened."

"Some cowboy may start wearin' diamonds," grinned Hashknife. "They won't be easy to dispose of in this country."

"Whoever got 'em can afford to wait for a chance to turn 'em into money — and they might wait a long time."

Hashknife liked Slim Caldwell. He seemed to have a lot of common sense. But Hashknife was more interested in old Rance McCoy. They had told Hashknife about Chuckwalla, and he sounded rather interesting. While the robbery of the express safe held certain elements of mystery, Hashknife was not greatly interested in it — not yet.

It rather amused him to think that the sheriff, prosecuting attorney, and the Wells Fargo representative believed that old Rance McCoy robbed the train, but because of the great amount of money involved, they hesitated to charge him with the crime.

He wondered why Kid Glover traded horses with him. It looked as though the Kid, traveling fast, crippled his horse and was obliged to make a quick trade. But why had the Kid been traveling fast, he wondered? And why did Butch Reimer deny any knowledge of that bay horse when Chuck Ring and Scotty McKay had been able to identify it instantly? Hashknife decided that the thing to do was to find out something about Kid Glover.

CHAPTER
FOURTEEN

Rance's Confession

"Of all the exasperatin' old badgers I ever did see, you're the worst, Rance."

Chuckwalla Ike sloshed a shirt up and down in a pan of soapy water and glared at Rance McCoy, who was tilted back against the kitchen wall, his heels hooked over the rung of a chair.

Rance made no reply to Chuckwalla's outburst, and it made Chuckwalla mad to be ignored. He yanked viciously on one side of his long mustache with a soapy finger and thumb, which caused the mustache to curl up in a dripping ringlet.

"Why in hell don'tcha try to find out where yore horse and saddle is?" demanded Chuckwalla. "Don'tcha care? Is the Circle Spade so dam' rich that yuh can lose a horse and saddle every once in a while and not miss it?"

The old man continued his thoughtful scrutiny of the old kitchen floor, ignoring Chuckwalla's outburst. Finally he lifted his head and looked at Chuckwalla, who was wringing the shirt.

"I heard somethin' about that horse," he said slowly.

"Yuh did, eh?"

"Uh-huh. I reckon me and you are about the only folks around here that don't know it. Jim Langley talked to me today about it."

Chuckwalla hung the shirt over the back of a chair and seated himself in the chair, facing Rance.

"Yea-a-ah?" he queried drawlingly. "And now I'm the only one that don't know. Jist about what are you talkin' about, Rance?"

"That holdup, Chuckwalla. Jist outside the railroad fence they found my horse and saddle the mornin' of the robbery. Horse had been shot. Yuh see, the messenger fired several shots."

Chuckwalla fingered his mustaches violently.

"That's shore clear to me," he said. "Yore horse and saddle? Say, Rance, where was you that night?"

"Don't go barkin' at shadders," advised Rance.

"A-a-aw, damn yuh, Rance; I didn't mean that. Can't yuh prove where yuh was?"

"Nope. Anyway, nobody asked me — yet. Remember that Slim and his two deputies ate breakfast with us that mornin'? They'd jist found the horse and saddle."

"Well, why didn't they arrest yuh, Rance?"

"Because they don't know where I cached that money."

"Well, I'll be damned!"

"And as long as I can't come out and tell where it is, they're scared to arrest me. Anyway, that's what Jim Langley told me; and he got it from Merkle."

Chuckwalla tugged at his mustaches, his eyes half-closed in deep meditation.

"What's yore opinion, Chuckwalla?" asked Rance.

126

"Don't never tell, Rance."

"I won't," Rance assured him warmly.

"That's the stuff. Didja see Angel in town?"

"I didn't see him, but he's there. The Eagle is closed."

"I'll betcha. You shore took the conceit out of him, Rance."

"Did I?"

"And close to eight thousand along with it. Take off that shirt and I'll wash it for yuh. Say, didja meet them two strange punchers?"

Old Rance peeled off his shirt and handed it to Chuckwalla.

"Yeah, I met 'em."

"So did I. That tall feller ain't nobody's fool. Me and him sets down on the sidewalk, and it ain't more'n five minutes before I finds m'self tellin' him all about you and Angel and Lila. Fact. Yuh hadn't ought to wear a shirt so long, Rance. Not over six weeks, at the outside.

"I dunno what this Hartley wanted to know so much for, and he didn't tell me. He looks plumb through yuh. Three times I started to lie to him — and quit. He talked with Angel. Yeah, he told me he had. Jim Parker took sort of a likin' to him and his pardner and invited them up to supper. I heard that Stevens won two hundred dollars at the Red Arrow Saloon the other day.

"I'll never git that neck-band clean, Rance. If you'd wash yore neck once in a while —"

"What did this Hartley person want to know?" interrupted Rance.

"Oh, jist a few things. F'r instance, he wanted to know how it comes that you have seventy-five hundred dollars, win close to eight thousand more — and then have to borrow money from the bank."

Chuckwalla sloshed the shirt around in the water and held it off at arm's length, looking at it critically. Old Rance peered at Chuckwalla, his grizzled eyebrows almost concealing his eyes.

"He asked yuh that, did he?" coldly.

"Shore."

"What did yuh say?"

"Nothin'. What *could* I say? I didn't know yuh did, Rance."

"I didn't know that things like that was anybody's business!"

"They are, when yuh git famous, Rance."

"Famous, eh?"

"Or notorious."

"That's a better word. I'm goin' to town, Chuckwalla."

"Thasso? Mebby I'll go with yuh."

"You better stay here, I think."

"Yuh think so, do yuh?" Chuckwalla wiped his soapy hands on his overalls and spat thoughtfully.

"I think so," nodded Rance.

"You think ag'in, Rance. You're aimin' to make a fool of yoreself, old-timer. Oh, I can read yuh like a book."

"I'm not goin' to start anythin', Chuckwalla."

"I know. That's jist yore polite way of sayin' that yuh won't shoot anybody from behind. You jist wait until I wring out them two pairs of socks and I'll be with yuh."

Hashknife seemed to make no effort to find out more about Kid Glover. He and Sleepy were content to lazy around the town, spending much of their time at the sheriff's office. They had met and talked with Lila, and Hashknife had talked at length with Angel, whom he found to be rather cynical and sarcastic. Hashknife put him down as a "bad boy." He liked Lila.

He found out that Billy DuMond was the one who had started the trouble in the McCoy family, and he tried to pump DuMond, but without any success. DuMond felt that he had already talked too much for the sake of his health.

Slim Caldwell was making no progress toward the solving of the robbery. The Wells Fargo man was still in town, possibly waiting for something to turn up. Hashknife did not bother to talk with him. Merkle wanted Rance McCoy behind the bars, and did not conceal his wishes.

Butch Reimer had not been in town since Hashknife and Sleepy had arrived, but on the morning that old Rance and Chuckwalla decided to come in, Butch, DuMond, and Dell Blackwell came to Red Arrow.

Slim Caldwell and Hashknife were together in the Red Arrow Saloon when Butch and his two men came in. Hashknife thought Butch seemed a little surprised to meet him again. Butch's misplaced eyebrow drew down a little as he nodded to Hashknife and Slim. DuMond and Blackwell ignored them entirely.

"How are yuh comin', Butch?" asked Slim casually.

"Oh, all right," grunted Butch. "Fair enough, I reckon."

129

"Where's Kid Glover?" asked Slim.

Butch frowned slightly, but answered readily enough: "The Kid pulled out a few days ago. I dunno where he went."

"I wish I did," said Hashknife, leaning one elbow on the bar and looking directly at Butch.

"Thasso?" queried Butch. "Why?"

"On account of my gray horse."

"Yea-a-ah? What about yore gray horse, Hartley?"

"I want him, Reimer. You say yuh don't know where Kid Glover is, eh?"

"No idea."

"And yuh didn't recognize that bay horse, didja?"

"What in hell is this — a guessin' contest?"

"Right now it is, Reimer. It may change any time."

Butch Reimer blinked slowly, thoughtfully. He knew he didn't stand a ghost of a chance to bluff this tall, gray-eyed cowboy.

"Why didja deny knowin' that bay horse?" asked Hashknife. "Lotsa folks recognized it as Kid Glover's horse."

"Did they?"

"That's a fact, Butch," said Slim softly.

"Uh-huh."

Butch cleared his throat harshly and tried to grin.

"I'll tell yuh why I didn't say anythin'," he explained. "I didn't know Hartley. The Kid was with me a long time, and yuh don't usually throw down folks yuh know in favor of a stranger, Slim. At least, I don't. I'll admit that the animal belongs to the Kid. He quit his job and pulled out of the country ridin' that bay horse.

130

Naturally, I didn't want to put him in bad; so I said I didn't know the horse."

The explanation was not entirely satisfactory to Hashknife.

"He must 'a' been in a hurry," said Hashknife.

"I dunno a thing about it," said Reimer testily. "I've admitted that I know the horse; what more do yuh want?"

"The horse."

"Well, I ain't got it!"

Butch shoved away from the bar and grew interested in the play at a roulette wheel. Hashknife smiled thinly, as he and Slim went back to the office, where they found Sleepy, Scotty McKay, and Jim Langley talking about the robbery.

"Even if a man had them diamonds — what could he do with 'em?" asked Langley. "Yuh can't sell 'em."

"Can't yuh?" laughed Scotty. "I could, y'betcha. I'd hop a train and take 'em East. You shore can sell diamonds in any big town."

"Yuh could do that, Scotty."

"Probably have to discount 'em pretty bad; but, at that, you'd have more money than yuh ever seen before."

None of them saw Rance McCoy and Chuckwalla Ike ride in. They tied their horses and went straight to the bank. Michael Hale, the cashier of the bank, nodded pleasantly at old Rance, but got a scowl in return.

"You told Merkle that I borrowed money, Hale," said old Rance accusingly. "I didn't know that was the way yuh done business."

131

Hale swallowed heavily. The old man's eyes were as hard as granite and the scars of his face showed white against the leather-brown of his skin.

"Why, I — I — he asked me about you," faltered Hale. "He wanted to know about your account here, and I — I told him you had closed it. He knew you lost twenty-five hundred, and he knew you drew —"

"And you told him I borrowed money, didn't yuh?"

"I — yes, I told him. He represents the law, and we —"

"That's all right, Hale. I jist wanted to tell yuh that yore bank won't never handle the money I stole from the Wells Fargo."

Old Rance turned on his heel and walked out, followed by Chuckwalla, leaving Hale to stare open-mouthed after them. Out on the sidewalk Chuckwalla turned fiercely on Rance.

"You old fool!" he snorted. "What didja say that for? Tellin' him yuh stole that money! My God, you're shore gettin' childish, Rance."

But Rance made no defense. He led the way to the courthouse and straight to Merkle's office. The officers of Red Arrow County had no office boys, no stenographers to bar the way of anybody who wanted to enter their sacred portals.

The Wells Fargo man was in conference with Merkle when Rance and Chuckwalla came in. Merkle took one look at the two old cattlemen and wished he was elsewhere.

"Hyah, lawyer," growled Rance, ignoring the other man. "Understand yuh been connectin' me with the

132

robbery of that train. I'm down here to make yuh put up or shut up. You're tellin' a lot of things about my business, Merkle. They tell me you're scared to arrest me, 'cause you're scared you'll never git the money back. And that's right, too. You slam me in jail and I'll never tell yuh where it is."

Merkle stared at the old man curiously. The Wells Fargo man seemed to see some humor in the situation, but said nothing.

"You — you admit doing it?" gasped Merkle.

"Don't need to, do I?" Rance laughed harshly.

"Will you sign a confession?"

"I'll sign nothin', Merkle. But I'll take a shot at you, as sure as hell, if yuh don't shut up about me. That's a fair warnin'. Put up or shut up."

"Why, I — I don't know what to say, McCoy."

"You've said about enough. C'mon, Chuckwalla."

They tramped out of the office and headed for the Red Arrow Saloon. Someone told Billy DuMond that Rance was on his way, and DuMond went out via the back door. He had no liking to meet Rance McCoy again.

And then old Rance and Chuckwalla proceeded to get drunk. The old man drank recklessly, which was unusual for him. Slim Caldwell heard that the two men from the Circle Spade were drinking heavily, and he also had a report from Merkle and Hale.

Merkle wanted Slim to arrest Rance at once.

"He admitted his guilt, sheriff. Regardless of the money end of the proposition, I demand his arrest. I'm not interested in the financial end of the thing, anyway.

133

He threatened me in my own office, and I have a witness. The sooner he's behind the bars the better it will be for all of us."

"Well," said Slim sadly, "I reckon there ain't nothin' else for me to do."

Jim Langley, Jess Fohl, and Roper Briggs had joined old Rance and Chuckwalla at the Red Arrow bar. Rance was getting drunkenly boastful.

"I've got 'em all fooled," he told Langley. "If they put me in jail, I'll never tell where the stuff is cached; sabe? Nossir, I'll never tell. Fill 'em up. Hundred and thirty-two thousand dollars. Sixty-seven thousand in jewlry and diamonds. Whooee-e-e! And I won't tell anybody where it is."

"You're an old fool," said Chuckwalla.

"F'r not tellin'?"

"For talkin' about it."

Fifteen minutes later, when Slim Caldwell arrested Rance, the old man stared drunkenly at him and then tried to pull his gun. It was little trouble for Slim to take the gun away from him and start him toward the jail. Chuckwalla leaned against the bar, talking to himself, trying to understand what had taken place.

He finally got it straight in his mind, and the knowledge that Rance McCoy was in jail sobered him up. He got his legs to functioning fairly well and headed for the office, where he found the sheriff's force, prosecuting attorney, Wells Fargo representative, Hashknife, and Sleepy.

"I've come to git him," stated Chuckwalla, and then added seriously, "And I git what I aim to git, gents."

"You better go home, Chuckwalla," advised Slim kindly.

"And leave Rance in jail?"

"Naturally."

"Well, you're a fool if yuh think so, Slim."

"Well, yuh can't get him out," declared Slim.

"Thasso?" Chuckwalla almost jerked out one side of his mustache. "Think I can't, eh? I'll show yuh! Betcha forty dollars I do git him out. I'll take him out if I have to dinnymite the dam' jail. Don't git me mean, gents."

"Go on home and shut up," advised Slim.

Hashknife took Chuckwalla by the arm and led him away, trying to explain that nothing could be done for Rance just now.

"But he never held up no train," wailed Chuckwalla. "Rance ain't that kind."

"Admits it, don't he?"

"Yea-a-a-ah! Old fool! Oh, I dunno what to do."

"You better go home and think it over, Chuckwalla."

"Mebby I better. Say, they'll take care of him, won't they?"

"Fine."

"Uh-huh. But I'm goin' to git him out, jist the same."

Chuckwalla managed to mount his horse, and Hashknife gave him the lead-rope to Rance's mount, explaining that there was no use of keeping the horse in town.

"You tell that Slim Caldwell that I'm comin' back," said Chuckwalla. "I'm a man of m' word, by God."

135

Jim Langley and his two men were at the office when Hashknife returned, and there was considerable speculation over what Chuckwalla Ike might do.

"He's a tough old rooster," laughed Langley. "Yuh never can tell about his kind."

"He won't do anythin'," declared Slim. "And old Rance won't never tell anything. Yuh may convict him, Merkle, but you'll never find that money. It's a big mistake, arrestin' him, anyway."

"That may be; but I'll take the chance. What else can I do?"

Later on in the day Butch Reimer ran into Slim, and they discussed the arrest of Rance McCoy.

"I hope yuh didn't think I was tryin' to block the wheels of justice when I didn't identify that horse," said Butch.

"It was all right, under the circumstances," said Slim. "I kinda wondered, after the horse had been identified."

"Hartley got kinda salty, didn't he?"

"Mebby. Yuh see, it was his horse, Butch."

"Yeah, I know it was. But don't yuh know, he made me a little bit sore. He's kinda inclined to be cocky, ain't he, Slim?"

"I don't think so. And it might be worth yore while to know that he's a bad jigger to get funny with, Butch."

"Yeah? How do you know all this? Did he tell yuh?"

Slim shook his head quickly.

"He'd be the last one to do that, Butch. I merely know these things from his reputation."

"Uh-huh. Got a reputation, eh? Gun-man?"

"Nope; not exactly. But he's shore sent a lot of gun-men down the trail. Didja notice them gray eyes of his? He looks plumb through yuh. If he ever asks yuh a question yuh better give him a square answer, Butch. Pity Kid Glover, if he ever comes back here again."

"I guess that's right," nodded Butch. "Do yuh reckon old Rance will confess?"

"No! All hell can't make him confess. And I don't see how Merkle can convict him on the evidence. There's not a thing, except that dead horse; and that ain't no real evidence. Of course, I don't know how the jury will look upon the fact that the saddle was recovered and the brands stripped off the dead horse. But they'll never get that money back — not a bit of it."

"I don't think they ever will," agreed Butch.

CHAPTER
FIFTEEN

Escape

That night Jim Parker seemed unusually serious during supper. Lila noticed that he looked often at her, and there was a gloomy expression in his eyes. Lila knew Rance McCoy had been arrested, and she wondered if this had anything to do with Jim Parker's demeanor.

Mrs. Parker noticed it too, and finally she asked him if he felt well.

"Well enough, mother," he said slowly. "We had a meeting this afternoon — the school trustees."

Lila lifted her head quickly and Jim Parker was looking at her.

"It was two to one," he said heavily. "I done the best I could, Lila, but they voted me down. I hated to have to tell yuh, but they ask yuh to quit teachin'."

"To quit teaching my school?" said Lila, hardly believing her own ears.

Jim Parker nodded sadly.

"That's it, Lila."

"The very idea!" exclaimed Mrs. Parker. "Why, Jim?"

Parker shook his head.

"It was the things they've heard," he said. "They called Angel in on it. He repeated what was in that

138

letter. That made no difference to me — but they're kinda funny. And after Rance was arrested — they thought they'd change."

"That letter about my — my father and mother?" asked Lila, a catch in her voice.

"Yeah!" snorted Parker. "One of them old fools talked about heredity. What does he know about it? Oh, I did the best I could, Lila. You can stay right here and live with us until yuh know what yuh want to do. We'd sure like to have yuh, Lila."

"Heredity?" whispered Lila. "He meant that — my mother was insane. Oh, that's what he meant."

"Don't you believe it, honey," assured Mrs. Parker warmly. "Nothin' to it. I'd like to talk to them trustees."

"I talked to 'em," said Parker. "They're going to ask me to resign from the board. I'll be glad to, and I told 'em so."

Lila left the table and went to her room. Jim Parker filled his pipe moodily, and while Mrs. Parker was clearing off the table Slim Caldwell came. He had talked with one of the trustees about Lila, and Slim was mad.

Lila came down the stairs. Slim was almost incoherent in his wrath, and afraid Lila would blame him for the arrest of Rance McCoy.

"I staved it off as long as I could. I didn't want to do it, if only for your sake," he told her. "Merkle demanded his arrest, and there wasn't anythin' I could do, Lila. Right now I'm lookin' for Angel. He talked with them trustees. You heard him, Jim. He didn't need to say the things he did. The things old Rance has done for the fool!"

"He's his son," said Lila wearily.

"And blood is thicker than water," quoted Parker.

"Oh, it doesn't matter," said Lila — "I mean, about me. I'm sorry for him. I don't believe he ever robbed anybody."

"He practically confessed it," sighed Slim. "Told Hale he'd never put a cent of it in the bank."

"What does he have to say now?" asked Parker.

"Nothin'. Oh, he's sober now. He realizes what he's up against. Merkle tried to get him to talk, and he laughed at Merkle when Merkle told him he'd let him off easy if he told where the money was cached. Then he got mad and cursed Merkle up one side and down the other."

"Has Angel been down to see him?" asked Mrs. Parker.

"No. Oh, he probably will — if I let him. Mebby I won't. No use rubbin' it in on the old man. He'll have his hearing in a few days, and they'll bind him over to the next term of court. Merkle says he'll convict Rance."

"They tell me that old Chuckwalla was sore," said Parker.

"I guess he was! Swears he'll dynamite the jail."

"Well, look out for him, Slim," seriously. "He's capable of doing just that thing. What's this I hear about Kid Glover stealing Hartley's horse in Welcome?"

"It's true, Jim. The Kid left the Half-Box R and traded horses in Welcome. Nobody knows where he is now."

"Does Hartley expect him back?"

Slim smiled over the manufacture of a cigarette.

"Nobody knows, Jim. That tall cowboy listens all the time, and when he talks it's to ask questions. Pretty much of a human being, that Hashknife Hartley. Thinks a lot. Thinks about everything, I reckon. Well, I've got to be gettin' back, folks. I was so danged mad, I had to come over and blow off steam."

"Thank you, Slim," said Lila, trying to smile. "It was something that couldn't be avoided. We'll all live through it. It was hard to believe, at first, but now it doesn't matter so much."

"That's a good way to look at it," said Slim. "You know how I feel about it. If I had a school in my pocket, it'd be yours, Lila."

"And I appreciate it, Slim. Please don't tell Rance McCoy about it. He has troubles enough of his own now."

"I won't tell him, Lila. Be good, folks.

It was nearly dark when Slim opened the gate. A man was coming toward him, and he looked up to see Angel McCoy, evidently coming to the Parker home. Neither of them spoke. Angel reached for the latch of the gate, but Slim swayed in front of him. And without any preliminary motions of any kind, Slim smashed Angel square on the point of the chin with his right fist.

It was a knock-out punch, perfectly timed and executed. Angel simply folded up and went sprawling in the dust. Slim looked at him for several moments, turned and went on toward his office, trying to rub some feeling back into his right knuckles.

Angel was "out" for more than a minute. He finally got to his feet, braced himself against the fence, and waited for his mind to clear. He had intended having a talk with Lila, but just now his jaw was half-paralyzed and there was a chunk of skin missing from his closely shaven chin. As soon as his legs would permit of safe locomotion, he went back toward the main street.

It was about nine o'clock when Chuckwalla Ike came back to Red Arrow. He was cold sober and wanted to see Rance McCoy, but Scotty McKay, alone in the office, refused his request.

"I have an or-rder to let no one see him," said Scotty. "Ye might come tomorrow, Chuckwalla."

"Yeah, I might," agreed Chuckwalla, and went away. He had a drink at the Red Arrow, and it was there that he learned that Lila had been asked to resign as teacher of the Red Arrow school.

It took Chuckwalla quite a while to digest this information, because of the fact that the bartender tried to explain heredity, which neither he nor Chuckwalla knew anything about.

"Anyway," declared the drink-dispenser, "I hear them trustees decided that she wasn't the woman they wanted to teach the kids; so they fired her."

"I dunno what her ancestors have got to do with her learnin' the kids," said Chuckwalla sadly.

"Me neither. Have another drink?"

"I don't guess I will, pardner. See yuh later."

He left the Red Arrow and walked past a restaurant, where he saw Slim, Chuck, Hashknife, and Sleepy busily engaged in eating their supper. For several moments Chuckwalla debated with himself whether to go in and talk with them or not. He finally decided not to, and went on.

For the first time since he had been in Red Arrow Hashknife talked at great length with Slim Caldwell about the robbery. There seemed little doubt that old Rance McCoy had pulled the job, but there were certain phases of the case that made Hashknife doubt.

Slim told him all about it, and answered questions until he became more interested himself.

"I dunno what yuh expect to learn," he declared, when Hashknife wanted all the details of the gambling incidents of the night of the robbery.

Slim went back several days previous to the robbery and told of old Rance losing twenty-five hundred dollars in the Eagle.

"You don't think Angel had any hand in it, do yuh?" asked Slim.

"I'd hate to say that. But isn't Angel the one who needed the money? Went broke, didn't he?"

"And he's still broke, Hashknife."

"Are yuh sure?"

"Well, he closed up his place."

"And old Rance borrowed money from the bank."

"Sure. But couldn't that have been a bluff? Why, we all know he drew seventy-five hundred from the bank; and he busted the Eagle. Don't tell me he's broke."

"Don't look as though he would be. You say the express messenger picked up his gun and emptied it at the robber after the robber left the car?"

"Yeah. Of course, he was shootin' wild in the dark."

"And one of his bullets killed the horse, eh? That meant that the robber would have to walk."

"It ain't over two miles to the Circle Spade ranch. We were over there that mornin', and old Rance had a big bump on his head. Looks as though a horse might have spilled him. He didn't have much to say. We didn't mention the horse to him, but it looks as though him and Chuckwalla beat it right down there and tried to destroy the evidence. Anyway, somebody was there ahead of Scotty, and danged near shot him. They held him off until they skinned out the brand and got away with the saddle."

"Looked as though there had been two men, eh?"

"Prob'ly was."

"How about Chuckwalla the night of the robbery?"

"Pretty drunk; too drunk to do anything."

They finished their meal and wandered down to the Red Arrow. Business was not very brisk.

"Old Chuckwalla was here a while ago," offered the bartender.

"Sober?" asked Slim.

"So damned sober he refused a second drink."

"Have anythin' to say about Rance?"

"Don't think so."

"Where'd he go from here?"

"Dunno that either."

They sat down at one of the tables and had a smoke. Hashknife noticed that Slim's right hand was bruised and swollen a little, and that Slim kept it concealed as much as possible.

Later on they sauntered back to the office, which was in darkness.

"Scotty must 'a' gone to bed," said Chuck. "He's shore a sleepy son-of-a-gun."

The door was unlocked. They walked in and Slim headed for the table, intending to light the lamp, when he tripped and fell sprawling across the floor.

"Why don'tcha pick up yore feet?" laughed Chuck.

"Light the lamp!" snorted Slim, picking himself off the floor. "By God, I fell over somebody!"

Hashknife quickly scratched a match and stepped over to the table, where he lighted the oil lamp. Stretched out on the floor, between the table and the door, was Scotty McKay, with blood oozing from a bruise on his head.

As they stared at him he groaned and tried to lift himself up. Quickly they placed him on a cot, and Slim ran to the jail door, which was sagging open. The cell was empty — Rance McCoy was gone.

Slim came back and looked at Scotty, who was staring blankly at them and trying to feel of his head.

"Rance is gone," said Slim. "How bad are yuh hurt, Scotty?"

"What in hell happened?" asked Scotty painfully.

"What do you know?" asked Slim.

Scotty looked blankly around, shaking his head.

"I dunno, Slim. I'm all blood! Who hit me?"

"There's some whiskey in my desk, Chuck," said Slim.

Chuck got the bottle and gave Scotty a big drink. It brightened him up quickly.

"I was at the desk," he told them. "There was a noise outside near the door, so I went to see what it was. And then somethin' hit me, I guess. Gimme another dr-r-ink, Chuck."

Slim sighed and looked inquiringly at Hashknife, who was sitting on a corner of the desk, squinting thoughtfully.

"What do yuh make of it, Hashknife?"

Hashknife shrugged his shoulders.

"Chuckwalla Ike!" exclaimed Chuck. "By God, he kept his word!"

"Looks like it," agreed Slim slowly. "You better go with Scotty to the doctor's place and get that head all fixed up. Can yuh walk, Scotty?"

"I don't walk on me head," retorted Scotty. "I'll be all right, Slim. I might have it looked into, though."

"Judgin' from your looks, it'll be easy to look into," grinned Chuck. "C'mon, old Painted Face."

"And when yuh come back, stick around the office," ordered Slim. "I'm goin' out to the Circle Spade."

"And we'll go along," said Hashknife, after the two men had departed. "This makes me kinda curious."

"I hoped you'd go, Hashknife. I'm curious too."

CHAPTER
SIXTEEN

Lost — a Hat

"What do you think of it, Sleepy?" asked Hashknife, as they saddled their horses.

"Fine!" grunted Sleepy. "This is action, cowboy. When they start knockin' officers down and bustin' jail, I'm feelin' good."

They mounted their horses and rode out to the Circle Spade. There was a light in the bunkhouse, but none in the ranch-house. They dismounted and sneaked up to the bunk-house window, where they looked in and saw Monty Adams and Steve Winchell, humped over at a table, playing seven-up.

They walked back to the corral, where they sat down and debated what to do. Slim did not want to go to the ranch-house and make a search. It might be productive of a lot of trouble, especially at night.

And as they sat there in the shelter of the corral fence, a horse and rider came to the ranch, dismounted near them, turned the horse into the corral, carried the saddle to the stable, and then went to the ranch-house. It was Chuckwalla Ike. He lighted a lamp in the living-room and took it upstairs with him.

147

"Foxy old devil!" snorted Slim. "He was too wise to bring Rance out here. Now where do yuh suppose he took him? Not to the Half-Box R, nor to the JML. He wouldn't have had time to go to the JML. I'll bet he stocked a hide-out in the hills."

"No use lookin' for him at night," said Sleepy. "We might as well go back to town and wait for daylight."

"Yeah; and he won't be so easy to take ag'in," complained Slim. "Old Rance is a danged fine shot, and he knows every inch of this country."

They went back to their horses and rode to town. Scotty was in bed at the office, suffering quite a lot with his injured head, in which the doctor had taken three stitches. It meant that several days would elapse before Scotty would be wearing a hat again.

A search of the office showed that the keys to the main door of the jail and to the cell were missing. Slim had kept them in a drawer in his desk. Luckily Slim had one set of duplicates.

"It wasn't done by a stranger," smiled Hashknife. "The man who pulled that job knew where to find the keys."

"No; it was done by a friend, Hashknife," laughed Chuck. "A friend with a lot of cold nerve."

"And honest too," laughed Slim. "He kept his word."

They were out again at daylight. Slim's idea was to keep a sharp watch on Chuckwalla. He believed that sooner or later Chuckwalla would go to old Rance. But Slim knew old Chuckwalla would be very careful, especially if he had any idea that the officers suspected him.

In order to look over considerable territory, in case old Rance should be hiding out in the country between the Circle Spade and the Half-Box R, Hashknife and Chuck headed straight for the Half-Box R, while Slim and Sleepy took the road to the Circle Spade.

Chuck knew of an old place, half shack, half dugout, hidden away in the hills between the two ranches. It had at one time been the winter home of a wolfer.

"Just stumbled onto it one day," explained Chuck. "Yuh never could find it, unless yuh knowed just where to look. Old Rance might know where it is, and it would shore make a dinger of a hide-out."

They came to the rickety old bridge across the river, which was barely wide enough for two riders abreast. On the left-hand side of the bridge, about a quarter of the way across, lay a battered sombrero. Hashknife swung down and picked it up.

It was not a hat that would ordinarily be discarded, being a black Stetson, more trampled than worn. There was no name in it, except that of the maker. Chuck looked it over critically.

"Lotsa black Stetsons wore around here," he said. "Mebby some of Butch Reimer's punchers got drunk and lost it."

Hashknife dismounted and stepped over to the railing. Thirty feet below him was a dry-wash, with here and there a clump of stunted bushes, piles of drift. Farther to the right was the river, only about sixty feet across at this time of the year.

Suddenly Hashknife leaned forward, looking almost directly down. Lying against one of the old pilings,

149

half-hidden in a tangle of brush and drift, was the body of a man. Hashknife called Chuck, and together they looked down at it.

From that distance it was impossible to identify him, as he was partly covered by the bushes. They led their horses back to the end of the bridge and tied them to a tree, after which they worked their way down to the river level.

Chuck did not like dead men, so he allowed Hashknife to drag the body out of the tangle. It was Billy DuMond. A round blue hole in the center of his forehead showed them that his death had been no accident. Chuck squatted down on his haunches and tore up several cigarette-papers in trying to roll a cigarette.

"Hit square between the eyes," he marveled. "Somebody around here is a damned good shot."

Chuck didn't pay much attention to Hashknife, who was examining the body, and he did not notice that Hashknife had taken some papers from DuMond's pocket. There were three envelopes, containing letters, which had evidently been carried a long time, and a folded sheet of paper.

Hashknife walked farther along under the bridge, as though searching for something more, and unfolded the sheet of paper. It was an inky scrawl, which read:

I.O.U. Seventy-eight hundred dollars.
($7800.00)

Angel McCoy

Hashknife stuffed the paper in his pocket and walked back to Chuck.

"What do yuh reckon we better do about this body?" he asked.

"Leave it here," said Chuck quickly. "Let Slim and the coroner handle it."

"Do yuh think we better ride down and tell Reimer?"

"Yeah, I s'pose we had. And then we can cut across the country and tell Slim. Who do yuh reckon killed old DuMond, Hashknife?"

"Somebody did a good job of it, Chuck. Who wanted to kill him off?"

"Rance McCoy."

"I heard about that. How did he stand with Angel?"

"Oh, all right, I guess. They seemed to be friendly. Yuh see, it was DuMond who told Angel about Lila not bein' Rance's daughter. I reckon that's what made Rance sore at DuMond. Yuh heard about Lila losin' her job, didn't yuh?"

"Yeah. That was a shame."

They went back to their horses and rode to the Half-Box R, where they found Butch Reimer and Dell Blackwell saddling their horses.

"Billy DuMond is dead!" blurted Chuck, without any preliminary.

Butch stared at him curiously.

"Dead?"

"Deader'n hell," forcibly, if inelegantly.

Butch dropped his latigo and came over to them. DuMond had been with Butch Reimer a long time.

151

"Yuh might tell me about it, Chuck," said Reimer, looking from Chuck to Hashknife.

Chuck told them how they had found DuMond, and that he had been shot squarely between the eyes. Butch was visibly affected, and it seemed to Hashknife that there was fear in his eyes, which shifted from face to face.

"If old Rance McCoy wasn't in jail —" he said, breaking off his sentence meaningly.

"Well, he ain't," said Chuck. "Somebody helped him break jail last night. They popped Scotty over the head."

Butch snorted disgustedly and hooked his thumbs over his belt.

"That accounts for it. Yuh won't have to look far for the man who killed Billy DuMond."

"Is Rance McCoy a murderer?" asked Hashknife.

"What do yuh mean, Hartley?"

"DuMond was murdered. His gun is still in the holster. The man who shot him shoved the gun almost against DuMond's head. And then he threw the body over the side of the bridge, hoping nobody would find it. But they made the mistake of leaving DuMond's hat on the bridge. Probably overlooked it in the dark."

Hashknife reached down inside his chaps and drew out the black Stetson, which he handed to Reimer. Hashknife was watching Reimer closely, and he saw his crooked lips twitch at sight of the hat.

Slowly he straightened it out in his two hands. Blackwell merely glanced at it. Butch cleared his throat softly.

"That's old Billy's hat," he said softly. "Poor old Bill."

"We better keep it," said Hashknife. "The sheriff will want to keep it, I suppose."

"What good is it to him?" queried Butch.

"Oh, merely a part of DuMond's personal effects. If yuh want it, Slim will probably give it to yuh."

"Well, all right," grudgingly. "Where's Slim?"

"Lookin' for Rance McCoy," replied Chuck.

"Same here," grunted Butch. "You tell Slim my gang are at his disposal. Jist as sure as hell, old Rance killed Billy DuMond. Do you think he's at the Circle Spade?"

"Not a chance. He's too smart for that. If you fellers are goin' to town, don't touch the body. We had to drag it out where we could look it over. As soon as we get hold of Slim, we'll have it taken to town."

Butch promised to keep away from it, and Hashknife rode away with Chuck, heading across the hills toward the Circle Spade. Hashknife was grinning to himself, and Chuck sensed the fact that Hashknife was amused.

"What's funny about it, Hashknife?"

"I was just laughin' to myself about Reimer wantin' to keep DuMond's hat as a souvenir."

"What's funny about it?"

"The fact that Reimer recognized it, Chuck."

"Well, he ought to recognize DuMond's hat, hadn't he?"

"Sure."

"Well, what's so funny about it?"

153

"Nothin' much, except that DuMond's head is not less than a seven and three-eighths, and this black hat is a six and seven-eighths."

"Yuh mean it ain't DuMond's hat?"

"Not unless that bullet swelled his head a lot."

"Well, I'll be damned!" exploded Chuck admiringly. "Slim was tellin' me you was smart. Who'd ever think of comparin' that hat with DuMond's head? I'll betcha Butch Reimer thinks it's DuMond's hat. Ha, ha, ha, ha, ha!"

"Anyway, he got kinda sentimental over it," grinned Hashknife. "Whereabouts is that dugout yuh mentioned?"

"Oh, that's north of us now. I thought we better find Slim first and tell him about DuMond."

"I guess so. Is that dead horse much out of our way?"

"Not much. We cross the railroad over here at Curlew Spur, and then we can foller up to where the horse is."

Fifteen minutes later they dismounted and looked at what was left of the Circle Spade horse. Coyotes and magpies had practically cleaned the bones of all flesh. Hashknife examined the skull of the animal, which was still covered with skin. The bullet had penetrated the animal's brain, and had gone through the skull. Hashknife examined the bullet-hole thoughtfully, and then walked to the fence and looked down at the tracks, which were at least twenty feet lower than where they stood.

"Make anythin' of it?" asked Chuck curiously. He was beginning to respect Hashknife's powers of observation.

"Sometimes yuh can make a mountain out of a molehill, Chuck," replied Hashknife gravely. "Mebby we better go and find Slim."

Slim had told them where to find him and Sleepy, and they were there, sitting in the shade of a stunted cottonwood, from where they had kept an eye on the Circle Spade ranch-house.

"Drawed a blank so far," grinned Slim. "Saw Monty and Steve ride away; but Chuckwalla ain't stirred."

"You tell 'em, Hashknife," said Chuck, as they dismounted.

Hashknife told Slim how they had discovered the body of Billy DuMond beneath the bridge, and the sheriff's eyes widened. He had known Billy DuMond a long time.

"Rance McCoy!" he gasped. "He's been gunnin' for DuMond. By God, he got loose, waited for Billy on that old bridge — and nailed him."

"Tell 'em about that hat," urged Chuck.

Hashknife grinned as he related the conversation between himself and Butch. He gave Slim the hat. They looked it over for identifying marks, but found none. The size was plainly marked on a sticker under the sweat-band.

"I never paid no attention to the size of DuMond's head," said Chuck.

"When yore life depends on noticin' things, yuh get the habit of seein' 'em," said Hashknife gravely. "Did any of yuh ever see old Rance McCoy wearin' a hat as big as this one?"

None of them had.

155

"It shore ain't the one he had when he was in jail," declared Chuck. "That one was an awful old wreck."

"Did Billy DuMond have any money?" asked Hashknife.

"On forty a month?" grinned Slim.

"Was him and Angel McCoy good friends?"

"Always have been, I reckon."

Hashknife straightened out the black sombrero. It was not the type of hat an old man would buy. It was one of the size known as "five-gallon," and of a rather expensive finish.

"Cost about forty dollars," said Hashknife. "I had one almost like it a few years ago. Wore it on Sunday. The jigger who owned this hat was kind of a dude."

"Which shore lets out Rance McCoy and Billy DuMond," laughed Slim. "I know DuMond wouldn't spend a month's salary for a hat. The question is — will we gain anythin' by waitin' for Chuckwalla to make a move?"

Hashknife shook his head slowly, still eyeing the hat.

"I don't think so, Slim. There's more behind this than we think. It's commencin' to brew a little. Crooks always make mistakes. And every time they try to rectify one, they make another. Don't believe what yuh see, because it might be made to look thataway."

Slim squinted closely at Hashknife, as though trying to read behind those level gray eyes.

"Hartley, have yuh struck a trail?" he asked.

"The makin' of one, Slim. The blazes ain't so danged plain yet — but they're blazes, just the same. Let's go back to town and get a rig to haul DuMond in with.

We'll let Chuckwalla do as he pleases to-day. If he had old Rance hid out in the brush, he wouldn't visit him in the daylight."

"That's right. We ain't got much sense."

"Not too much, Slim."

CHAPTER
SEVENTEEN

Kid Glover

"No such a thing! You're crazy, all of yuh!"

Old Chuckwalla fairly danced up and down on the sheriff's office floor and his mustaches bristled angrily. He shook a gnarled fist at Slim Caldwell.

"You long-legged gallinipper!" he roared. "You accuse me of bustin' yore hen-coop of a jail, do yuh? You think I let Rance McCoy out, eh? I'd shore crave to know where yuh got that idea."

It was the day after they had found DuMond's body, and Chuckwalla had just been told that Rance had been delivered from the jail. Slim had come out openly and asked Chuckwalla where he had taken Rance. Of course the old man was properly indignant.

"You swore you'd bust the jail," reminded Slim.

"Uh-huh. Shore I did. I was mad — and drunk. But I never done it, Slim. Honest to God!"

"Then where in hell is he?" demanded Slim. "If you didn't take him out — who did?"

Chuckwalla waved his arms helplessly.

"How'd I know?"

Slim turned and looked at Hashknife, who was smiling at old Chuckwalla.

"What do you think, Hashknife?"

"Oh, I dunno. You know Billy DuMond is dead, don'tcha, Chuckwalla?"

"Heard he was. That ain't nothin' to tear a shirt over. This country would 'a' been better off if DuMond had been strangled in infancy. Blame Rance for it, don'tcha? Sure, yuh would."

Chuckwalla glared indignantly and backed to the door.

"Where are yuh goin'?" asked Slim.

"To hunt for Rance McCoy. Somebody's got to find him — and the sheriff's office is full of incompetent chair-warmers."

"Where are yuh goin' to look?" asked Chuck.

"That's none of yore business."

He went up the sidewalk, tramping heavily, his spurs rasping on the worn boards. Slim shrugged his shoulders wearily and leaned back in his chair.

"Now, what do yuh think, Hashknife?"

"The old boy seemed very emphatic, Slim."

Hashknife walked to the door and looked up the street. He saw Lila enter Parker's store.

"I think I need some tobacco," he said, and left the office. Slim watched him out of the door, and saw him join Lila. He started to follow him, but decided not to.

He met Lila at the store entrance. She was taking some packages down to Parker's house; so he walked along with her.

"Things are breakin' kinda bad for yuh, ain't they?" asked Hashknife.

Lila nodded. It seemed to Hashknife as though she did not want to talk about it.

"You heard about DuMond's death?" he asked.

"Yes."

"Do yuh think Rance McCoy killed him?"

"Not if he was murdered, as they say he was. Rance McCoy would have killed him in a fair fight."

"They think Chuckwalla took him out of jail."

"I know they do. But I don't believe it. Chuckwalla talks a lot. He's just a big-hearted old man, rough on the outside. He wouldn't hit Scotty McKay, unless it was in a fair fight."

"You don't dislike Rance McCoy, do you?"

"Dislike him?"

Lila turned her head away, but not too quickly for Hashknife to have seen the tears in her eyes.

"I don't dislike him," she said wearily. "I was hurt and sick over it all. It seemed so unfair that no one had told me who I was — and what I was. You don't know what it means, Mr. Hartley. And now they've taken my school away."

"Yeah, I heard about it, Lila. I'm callin' yuh Lila because everybody else does."

"That's all right."

They stopped at the Parker gate.

"I've heard that Rance McCoy and his son never did hitch very well," said Hashknife.

"Not very well," admitted Lila. "They've always been at swords' points, even when Angel was a little boy. Rance McCoy has always stood by Angel, even when Angel deserved severe punishment, but there never

160

seemed any love between them. Even, when Angel and I were little, he used to take Angel's part against me."

"Case of blood bein' thicker than water, eh? Oh, I didn't mean to say that, Lila."

"But it is true."

"Yeah, I reckon it is."

"Do you believe in heredity?" Lila was painfully serious now. It was a question that hurt her to propound.

"Heredity? If yuh mean physical forms, color, disposition — yes. If yuh mean inherited vices, physical failings — no. Horse-stealin' don't necessarily run through a family. Preachers' sons don't usually make preachers. Blindness ain't inherited; so why should any other physical ailment be? I knowed two weak little folks up in Montana that raised a heavy-weight fighter. But yuh can make yore own heredity, Lila — most folks do."

"You mean — thinking about it?" anxiously.

"Thinkin' the wrong way about it."

"But — but what if other folks think against you?"

Hashknife laughed softly and shook his head.

"That's an Injun idea, Lila. Never admit that yore medicine is weaker than that of the other feller. Yore mind is the only one that can hurt you."

Lila sighed and shifted her packages.

"Anyway," she said, trying to smile, "your theory is worth thinking about."

"It's worth usin'," seriously. "I know, because I've shore used it. You quit worryin' about yourself — and

161

about anythin'. You've done no wrong; and when you're right, yuh don't need to worry about anythin'."

"Perhaps that is right. Oh, I hope everything will come out right for Rance McCoy. Slim Caldwell likes you; he told me he did."

"Well," grinned Hashknife, "that makes two folks he likes, Lila, 'cause he didn't need to tell me who the other one was."

Lila blushed quickly and hurried toward the house. At the porch she turned and waved to Hashknife, and he knew she was smiling.

He went back to the office, where the doctor was dressing Scotty's head. Slim had gone up the street, but Chuck and Sleepy were still there.

"Let's go down and take a look at the shack we didn't see yesterday," suggested Hashknife.

Chuck quickly agreed. They took a pair of rifles from the sheriff's gun-rack, saddled their horses, and headed out of town, after leaving word with Scotty to tell Slim where they were going.

They took the road which led to the Half-Box R, crossed the bridge where they had found DuMond's body, and then swung to the left, following the river. The country was very rough, and the buck-brush grew thick, with here and there a large patch of greasewood and occasional jackpine clump.

But Chuck knew the location of the hidden shack, and led them straight to it. There was no clearing to show that any kind of a habitation existed. The front end of the dwelling had been built of jack-pine poles, more like the entrance to a tunnel than a human abode.

The old door was still in place, but sagging open. Just at the entrance, where they dismounted, was a space of possibly twenty feet long of fairly bare ground. There were horse-tracks here, and Hashknife squatted on his heels to study them closely, while Sleepy and Chuck kept an eye on the sagging door.

"C'mere, Sleepy," said Hashknife. He pointed a forefinger at a track in the dusty earth. In fact there were two tracks close together, apparently made by the same animal, but one track showed a smooth shoe, while the other mark plainly showed a calked shoe.

"The Ghost!" snorted Sleepy. "Yessir, that's him."

"Yore gray horse?" queried Chuck.

"Yeah," nodded Hashknife.

"Yuh mean to tell me yuh know the footprints of yore own horse, Hashknife?"

"I ought to — I shoe him myself, Chuck. Notice that track? That's his left front foot. Put a toe-calk on that foot and he'll stumble badly; so I always shoe him with light calks on the rest, and leave that one plain. But the worst of it is, we don't know how long ago these tracks were made. A track would look fresh a long time in that dry earth."

Practically all of the cabin was a dugout, and, except for the entrance, was of dirt walls. The floor was of dirt. At the rear was a small fireplace, and the rusty old stovepipe barely cleared the top of the brush on the slope of the hill.

There had not been a fire in the dugout for a long time, and the only sign of occupancy was an empty bean can, still containing a few fairly fresh beans, and

163

on the dirt floor were a number of cigarette-butts. Hashknife examined them and decided that some of them had been smoked but a short time ago.

They came back to the sunlight and mounted their horses.

"Somebody's been here lately," decided Hashknife. "And that person ate canned beans, smoked cigarettes, and rode my horse. If Kid Glover stole my horse, and still rides him, he came back from Welcome instead of keeping on goin'."

"He'd probably know about this dugout," said Chuck. "The Kid was here quite a while, and lots of the Reimer stock range through here. I wish I knew why he stole yore horse, Hashknife. He probably don't know whose horse he got, and I don't think it would make any difference to him if he did. The Kid shore is a cold-blooded person, and if he's got any conscience at all, I'm an evangelist."

"Let's ride over to the Half-Box R," suggested Hashknife. "Butch Reimer might have some word of Glover."

"He wouldn't give the Kid away, Hashknife. But we'll ride over, anyway. Yuh never can tell."

But they were spared the ride. As they struck the road below the bridge they met Reimer and Blackwell, traveling toward town.

"Hyah, cowboys," grunted Butch. "What do yuh know?"

"Not much," smiled Hashknife. "Ain't seen anythin' of Kid Glover, have yuh?"

A queer expression flashed across Butch's eyes as he looked quickly at Hashknife.

"Haven't seen him; have you, Hartley?"

"Nope. But if he's ridin' my gray horse, he's been around here lately."

"How do yuh make that out?"

"Found the track of my horse."

Butch laughed shortly.

"Yuh don't mean to say yuh know the track of yore horse, do yuh, Hartley?"

"Yeah. Shod him myself, Butch."

"Oh, yeah."

Butch drew the brim of his hat farther down over his eyes as he looked out across the broken hills.

"Kinda funny, ain't it — him comin' back?"

"What's funny about it?" demanded Butch. "It's a free country."

"Pretty free," admitted Hashknife.

They bunched together and headed back toward Red Arrow. Hashknife would have given much to know what was going on behind Butch's little eyes, which seemed busy scanning the road and the surrounding country. There was little conversation. Hashknife was doing a bit of thinking himself. Blackwell talked to Chuck and Sleepy, but seemed to avoid Hashknife.

"Inquest to-morrow," said Hashknife, breaking a long silence between him and Butch.

Butch nodded shortly.

"Bury Billy in town, I reckon. Got no relatives that I know about. I hope they git old Rance."

"Think Rance shot him?"

"Sure. He was the only man who wanted to kill old DuMond."

"But he wanted to kill him fair, didn't he?"

"If he had a chance. Billy was scared of him."

"And you think Rance McCoy deliberately murdered him?"

"I reckon that's what the jury will say."

"I suppose they will."

After a few minutes of deliberation, Butch turned in his saddle and looked squarely at Hashknife.

"What do you think of it?" he asked.

"I dunno," evaded Hashknife.

"I jist wondered. You've had so dam' much to say about it. I believe in leavin' things like that to the sheriff and the court, and if the rest of the folks would do the same, we'd be better off."

"Some folks would," agreed Hashknife meaningly.

"Some folks would what?"

"Be better off."

"Mm-m-m-m."

Butch touched spur to his horse and moved in beside Chuck, leaving Hashknife to bring up the rear. But the tall, gray-eyed cowboy didn't seem to mind. He grinned widely and began rolling a cigarette.

Hashknife and Sleepy testified at the inquest on the following day, but the questions were perfunctory. There was no evidence to connect Rance McCoy with the killing; so the coroner's jury decided that Billy DuMond had been killed by a gun-shot wound, fired by a party or parties unknown. But they did recommend that the sheriff apprehend Rance McCoy.

Which was a rather ridiculous recommendation, as the sheriff already wanted Rance on the charge of robbing the Wells Fargo Express Company. Hashknife had asked Slim not to exhibit the black sombrero, and Slim respected Hashknife's wishes to the extent that no mention was made of the hat.

Reimer and his crew were there, but none of them made any mention of the hat. After the inquest Butch Reimer asked Slim who had the hat, and was informed that the hat was locked up in the office safe. Butch did not comment on it, nor did he ask just why Billy DuMond's hat should be locked up in a safe.

Billy DuMond's body was duly interred that day, and there were no mourners. Butch Reimer paid the preacher and the doctor, who acted in the capacity of undertaker, and Billy DuMond was consigned to what was known as the "Red Arrow Cemetery" — the wind-swept slope of a hill surrounded with greasewood.

"I'm goin' to git the man who shot Billy," Butch Reimer was heard to declare, and every one knew he meant Rance McCoy.

"You better not announce yore approach," grinned Jim Langley, who came in for the inquest. "He's one hard old jigger."

Langley had Jess Fohl with him. Jess drank quite a lot of liquor before the funeral, and cried all the way back to town, where Langley told him he'd cut his ears off if he took another drink. Langley came down and talked with Slim and Hashknife about old Rance. Langley did not seem to think that Rance shot

DuMond, but he would not even venture a guess as to who had killed him.

"Why don'tcha think it was Rance?" queried Hashknife.

"It's like this," explained Langley. "Rance got that hundred and thirty-two thousand dollars cached. Chuckwalla busted jail for him, and old Rance has high-tailed it out of this country, takin' the stuff along. As soon as things blow over, old Chuckwalla will hit the grit. Now, you jist watch and see if I ain't right, Slim."

"And you think Rance was so anxious to get out of the country that he wouldn't stop long enough to kill DuMond, eh?" asked Hashknife.

"I don't think he would."

"And you don't think old Rance will ever come back?"

Langley shut his lips tightly for a moment, as he shook his head in the negative.

"No," he said, "I'd almost bet he won't."

"Well, we better work on it from a different angle, Hashknife," said Slim seriously.

"Are you workin' on it, Hartley?" asked Langley.

"Well, I'm kinda helpin' Slim," laughed Hashknife.

Later on that day Langley and Butch Reimer met in front of the Red Arrow and discussed the case. Reimer had imbibed a few drinks and was inclined to be big-voiced.

"What we need is a sheriff who can arrest and hold a man," he said. "Slim's all right in his way, but he don't weigh enough. Ha, ha, ha, ha, ha!"

Langley laughed with him.

168

"Slim's got a feller workin' with him who's jist a little skinnier than Slim," laughed Langley.

"Oh, that Hartley person. Don't look like much, does he, Jim? But lemme tell yuh somethin'." Butch grew very confidential. "Slim says this feller is a wonder as a detective. Accordin' to Slim, this Hartley's got a nose that can smell out crime like a bloodhound follerin' boot-tracks in the snow."

"Is he a detective?" asked Langley.

"And then some, accordin' to Slim."

"Well," said Langley seriously, "yuh never can tell much about a man, lookin' at him from the outside. But Slim is goin' to need more than a thin-faced puncher to clear up all this mess."

"That's true. Say, have yuh seen anythin' of Angel lately?"

"He's workin' for me," laughed Langley. "Quite a drop, eh? Well, he was kinda sour on the world, Butch, and jist for fun I offered him a job. He's busted, he says. Old Rance cleaned him out that night, I reckon. He's a good puncher. For some reason he's sore at Slim."

"On account of that girl," said Butch. "They're both stuck on her."

"Shucks!" exclaimed Langley. "She was the one who busted up Angel's games that night. She swore he was crooked. He wouldn't want her, Butch."

"Mebby not; I was jist guessin'; but Slim sure does. Where do yuh suppose old Rance is hidin' out?"

"He ain't hidin'; he's foggin'. Betcha ten to one he never comes back, Butch."

169

"No, I wouldn't bet on it, Jim."

"How much do yuh want to bet?"

They turned quickly to face Hashknife, who had come up behind them unnoticed.

"Why, I — I dunno," faltered Langley. "How much do yuh want to bet, Hartley?"

"Anywhere from a hundred to a thousand — at one-to-ten, Langley. It looks like easy money to me."

Hashknife had exactly fifty dollars in his pocket. If it hadn't been that Sleepy's luck had been good at the Red Arrow, both of them would have been broke by this time.

But Langley wouldn't bet, and Hashknife had been sure of it. He knew Langley's type very well.

"Anyway," declared Langley, "that's my personal opinion. I may be wrong, of course. But why would *you* bet on a thing like that, Hartley?"

"I'd bet that the moon was made of cheese if somebody would give me odds like that. And I really think he'll come back, Langley."

"Well," dubiously, "you may be right. He'd be a fool to come back, I think, don't you?"

"Looks thataway to me," agreed Butch. "I wouldn't."

Langley had some purchases to make, so he excused himself and went down to Parker's store, leaving Butch and Hashknife together.

"Jim just told me that Angel is punchin' cows for him," said Butch.

Hashknife smiled. "I wondered where he'd gone."

"The old man busted him, Hartley. By golly, the old man sure went out of this country well heeled. He can afford to lose his ranch. I'll be danged if I think he'll ever come back. I'd hate to even take Langley's ten-to-one bet on a thing like that."

"Well, I'll take it, Reimer. And if Kid Glover ever shows up at yore place, I wish you'd let me know. I want that gray horse, and I won't go hard with the Kid. He merely traded with me, and I'll consider that he's over bein' colorblind."

Butch smiled grimly.

"I'll tell him, Hartley. But do yuh really think he was back in this country?"

"I'd know them hoof-marks in hell. And if he was headin' out of the country, he wouldn't come back here from Welcome, just to make tracks in the dust."

"No, that's a fact. But lemme tell yuh somethin', Hartley; if you meet Kid Glover, shoot quick. He's a bad man, and if he knows you own that horse, he'll kill yuh when yuh meet."

"Oh, I'm not worryin' about that, Reimer; but thanks, just the same."

"You're welcome."

"He's kinda goin' back on his own friends," said Hashknife to himself, as he went back to the office. "Warns me to shoot first, eh?"

Slim wanted to go down across the river and watch the old dugout, but Hashknife had no liking for that tangle of brush at night, so they decided to make it an early morning call instead. Slim had sent out telegrams describing old Rance McCoy, warning the officers of the neighboring counties to be on the lookout for him; but as yet no one had reported seeing him.

171

It was about midnight that night, and Hashknife and Sleepy were in their room talking over the events of the day. The town was very quiet when they heard a horse running up the street, a splattering of hoof-beats, denoting that the rider had, in the parlance of the range, "spiked his horse's tail" across the street from them at the Red Arrow Saloon.

Hashknife cautiously blew out the lamp before raising the window and shade. Excited voices showed that something had excited them. He could see a horse and several men in the light from the saloon window. One man ran down the street toward the sheriff's office, while another headed the opposite way.

"We better go down and listen to this, Sleepy," said Hashknife. They drew on their boots and headed for the saloon. Slim was just arriving on the scene, pulling on his shirt.

Dell Blackwell, of the Half-Box R, was the rider.

"Now tell me jist what happened," said Slim, half out of breath.

"Somebody shot Eddie Corby. Here's the way it was. Me and Butch and Jim Kendall and Eddie was playin' poker in the bunk-house. Butch was losin', and he got so mad he tore up the cards. He always does that. Well, we didn't have another deck in the bunk-house.

"Butch said he had several decks in the ranchhouse, but he'd be damned if he'd go after one. Eddie said he'd get it, and Butch told him they was in a cupboard in the front room. Eddie was gone jist a few minutes when we hears a gun go off.

"We busted out to see what was goin' on. We was all kinda jumpy since DuMond got shot, yuh see. But there wasn't nothin' to be seen, because it was dark as hell. There's a light in the house, and we all went up there. The front door is wide open, and there in front of that cupboard lays Eddie, shot from behind.

"I think he's dead, m'self; but Butch says to bring a doctor. Looks t' me as though he'd been shot with a thirty-thirty, and I don't think he's got a chance in the world. And that's all we know about it, Slim."

"Why would anybody shoot Eddie Corby?" wondered Slim Caldwell.

Corby was an inoffensive sort of person, who was not physically strong enough to be a cowboy; so he worked as a horse-wrangler and helped around the ranch.

"It's got me beat," declared Blackwell. "Eddie never done anythin' to anybody. Why, he hardly ever went off the ranch. Personally, I think somebody mistook him for Butch. They're about the same size, and Butch is the only one who sleeps in the ranch-house. I wouldn't tell this to Butch, 'cause it'd scare hell out of him."

"Who'd shoot Butch?" asked Slim quickly.

"Who knows? Butch might have enemies, Slim."

"I suppose he might. I'd better saddle up. When the doctor shows up, tell him I'm goin' out. Mebby I'll beat him there. Want to go along, Hashknife?"

Hashknife shook his head quickly.

"You don't need me, Slim."

"I'll take Chuck. I left him tryin' to get his legs out of his coat-sleeves. Made a mistake and grabbed his coat instead of his pants."

Hashknife and Sleepy went back to the hotel.

"What's gone wrong with this country?" asked Sleepy. "Ain't they got *no* respect for human life?"

"Not in their frame of mind. From now on, look out. When they start playin' this here tit-tat-toe stuff with bullets, yuh never know when you're goin' to be 'it.' I don't like the rules they use."

"What do *you* know?" demanded Sleepy.

"Guessin' a little, Sleepy."

"Yea-a-ah? Who shot this Corby person?"

"That's a pretty blunt question, cowboy. We better hit the hay and catch up a little sleep."

"Say!" demanded Sleepy. "Why won't yuh never let me in on anythin' yuh know?"

"Dunno anythin'. Do you believe in heredity?"

"I sure do, you descendant of a clam."

It was after daylight the next morning when they brought in the body of Eddie Corby, but Hashknife was not there. He had ridden away from Red Arrow an hour before daylight, alone, leaving Sleepy to look and listen to everything that happened in town.

Sleepy protested against this, but Hashknife usually had his way in matters of this kind. He rode straight to the Circle Spade, where he found Chuckwalla Ike just starting to cook breakfast. The old man looked Hashknife over quizzically, but invited him to eat with them.

"Ridin' early, ain'tcha?" he asked.

"It's nice to ride early," smiled Hashknife. "Ain't nobody liable to bushwhack yuh early in the mornin'."

"Are you expectin' to be bushwhacked, Hartley?"

"Somebody killed Ed Corby at the Half-Box R last night."

Chuckwalla frowned heavily and caressed his mustache.

"Killed Ed Corby?"

"Shot him in the back. Understand that somebody shot through an open door. Anyway, I guess he's dead. Blackwell brought the news about midnight. He came after the doctor, but he said he was sure Corby was dead."

"Well, I'll be damned! Ed Corby! I don't make sense out of that. Corby was a harmless sort of a jigger. Wasn't very well. I'll be damned! Probably lay that onto Rance McCoy."

Hashknife sprawled on a kitchen chair and rolled a cigarette, while Chuckwalla, muttering to himself, went ahead with his breakfast preparations.

"I came to talk with yuh about Rance McCoy," said Hashknife.

Chuckwalla turned quickly, as though on the defensive.

"What about?"

"I want the truth."

"The hell yuh do! Well, now —"

"Don't flare up," said Hashknife. "If you turned Rance McCoy loose, it's all right with me. I've got a pardner, Chuckwalla, and I'd bust any jail on earth to get him out. What you tell me won't go any further — but I want to know the truth."

Chuckwalla flung a frying-pan on the stove and came back to face Hashknife.

"I didn't bust that jail!" he snorted. "Lot of you fools won't believe me, eh? Well, don't! I don't ask yuh to. I want to find Rance McCoy as bad as you do — mebby worse. Now, what do yuh think of that?"

"I believed yuh the first time, Chuckwalla. Now, let me ask you a question. Why did Rance McCoy borrow money from the bank a few days ago?"

"Did he? He never told me. Why, he had money. Didn't he bust the bank at the Eagle? Shucks, I don't believe he borrowed money."

"Did yuh ever know Billy DuMond to have a lot of money?"

"Hell, no! Never got over forty a month since I knowed him."

"When I found his body," said Hashknife slowly, "I found a paper in his pocket. It was an I.O.U. for seventy-eight hundred dollars, signed by Angel McCoy."

"Ha-a-a-aw?" Chuckwalla gawped at Hashknife blankly.

"I've still got the paper, Chuckwalla."

"Hell's delight!" Chuckwalla yanked viciously at his mustache. "How could Angel borrow seventy-eight hundred from DuMond — unless —"

"Unless what?"

"Unless DuMond robbed that train."

"Yeah, he might," reflected Hashknife. "It was the same amount they tell me Rance McCoy won from Angel."

"By God, that's right! Mebby DuMond loaned him that much. But DuMond is dead and he can't never collect. I'll bet Angel's glad. He's the kind who would be glad."

"You ain't got much use for Angel, eh?"

"The pup! Rance ort to have wrung his neck when he was young. He shore caused Rance plenty grief."

"What did Rance think about Lila leavin' him?"

Chuckwalla shook his head slowly and turned back to the stove.

"That hurt him, Hartley. He didn't say much, but I know him pretty well. He loved Lila. I reckon she's about the only thing he did love, and she turned him down jist because he never did tell her who she was. She hadn't ort to have done that. Queer idea, 'pears to me."

"What do you know about her parents?" asked Hashknife.

"No more than you do. He never told me anythin'. Even after Billy DuMond talked about it, old Rance never did explain anythin." But I seen tears in his eyes one night. And the old fool was readin' a book upside down. Don't let anybody tell yuh he ain't got feelin's."

"But who do yuh think busted the jail for him?"

"Probably busted it himself. Mebby they forgot to lock him in. That dam' sheriff's force! I'd like to see one of the old-time sheriffs ag'in. They'd keep their man, y'betcha."

Chuckwalla stepped outside and hammered lustily on an old triangle with a piece of drill-steel, calling Monty Adams and Steve Winchell to breakfast.

The two sleepy-eyed cowboys exhibited no surprise at finding Hashknife at breakfast. Chuckwalla told them about Ed Corby's death, and they marveled exceedingly.

"What's new about Rance?" asked Steve. "We're gettin' kinda anxious about the old man, Hartley."

Hashknife could tell them nothing.

"Yuh don't need to worry about yore pay," said old Chuckwalla. "The Circle Spade is worth it."

"Who's worryin'?" flared Steve. "We'd sooner work for our board for Rance McCoy than to get a raise at any other ranch."

"Yuh ought to — he lets yuh do as yuh please."

"Can yuh imagine a disposition like that?" queried Monty. "Chuckwalla, you ought to have rattles, like a snake; you've got the disposition of one."

The old man chuckled over his pans. He delighted in rough sarcasm.

Hashknife left right after breakfast. Chuckwalla came out to his horse and shook hands with Hashknife.

"I hope yuh can get some track of Rance," he said. "I tell yuh, I'm worried about the old man."

"It's time somebody got worried about him," said Hashknife.

He rode back almost to the river and then turned southwest, intending to take another look at the old dugout, and wondering if he could find it again. He felt sure he could come in from the opposite direction and find it.

Hashknife traveled slowly and cautiously, trying to pick up some of the landmarks he had noticed when they were in there before. Down among the breaks he struck an old cattle-trail, which he felt would lead him fairly close to the dugout, but it split up at an old water-hole in a brushy coulee.

There were plenty of Half-Box R cattle in that part of the range, many of them as wild as deer. Hashknife worked his way back to the top of a rocky ridge, where he dismounted and made a cigarette. The breeze was from the west, and before his cigarette was rolled his nose caught a peculiar scent.

He lifted his head quickly, sniffing at the breeze. It was the unmistakable scent of frying bacon. Somewhere in that tangle of hills, and not far away, somebody was cooking breakfast.

Hashknife tied his horse behind an outcropping of granite boulders, and began working his way slowly ahead, stopping often to sniff at the breeze. He was obliged to travel a crooked course, winding around the upthrusts of granite, the tangle of greasewood and sage.

Now he could smell wood-smoke, mixed with the odor of coffee, but it was evident that the cook was using very dry wood which made little or no visible smoke. Suddenly Hashknife stopped short and leaned in close to a boulder. Just ahead of him in a little clearing was a man, squatting at a tiny fire. He had his back to Hashknife, as he ate from a small frying-pan, and drank from a tin can, which flashed back the rays of the sun.

The man was bareheaded. Around his throat was a dirty-white handkerchief. He wore no coat nor vest over his faded blue shirt, and his broad, bat-wing chaps seemed fairly new. The sun glinted on the heads of the cartridges in his belt, and a heavy gun sagged from his holster. His hair appeared very black at that distance.

Just behind him was a bright-colored blanket, spread out on the ground, and on it lay a rifle and several odds and ends. Finally he shook the coffee grounds from the can and poured the grease from the pan. Placing the two utensils together, he stamped out the fire with a thrust of his foot, hitched backwards to the blanket, where he began rolling a cigarette.

It seemed to Hashknife that the man would never turn around. He leaned back on one elbow and smoked slowly, apparently taking his ease. Magpies chattered at him from a tall greasewood across the coulee. They had evidently scented food.

Suddenly a horse nickered, fairly close at hand. Like a flash the man was on his feet, crouched, his head swinging from side to side, as he scanned the hills to the north and west. Then he whirled around and looked in Hashknife's direction, but Hashknife had thoughtfully flattened himself against the rock.

Then the man stooped quickly, scooped up the blanket, took his cooking-utensils, and faded into the brush, like a shadow. But Hashknife had seen his face, and it was no one he had ever seen before. The man was dark, thin-faced, with rather a long neck. His hair was very straight and appeared coarse, curving down over his forehead in a decided mat. He was about five feet, ten inches tall, but would not weigh more than a hundred and twenty-five.

After his sudden disappearance Hashknife relaxed and watched across the coulee. It was possibly five minutes later that he saw two riders, going slowly through the brush, about a hundred yards north of him. It was Jim Langley and Angel McCoy. As far as Hashknife could judge from their actions, they were not looking for anybody.

They passed out of sight, heading toward the Circle Spade ranch. But Hashknife held his position, and in a few minutes he saw a rider cutting along the side of a hill below him — a bareheaded man, riding a tall, gray horse. He was looking back, as though watching Langley and Angel. Finally he turned and rode deeper into the cañon.

Hashknife grinned slowly and went back toward his horse.

"So that's Kid Glover, eh?" he mused to himself. "He's a tough-lookin' hombre, and he's still ridin' Ghost. And he'll just about stick around here until I trade horses with him — and have one more horse than I've got now."

CHAPTER
EIGHTEEN

Hashknife at Work

Hashknife rode across to the bridge and headed back to Red Arrow. The news of Ed Corby's death had flashed over the range, and many men came in to look at him and to wonder why anybody should shoot an inoffensive man like Corby.

Butch Reimer was in town and Hashknife met him at the sheriff's office. There was no question about Butch being nervous over the killing of Corby. He had lost his usual air of bravado. Sleepy told Hashknife that Butch had asked about him as soon as he came to town, and Sleepy had led him to believe that Hashknife was still in town.

Sleepy had little else to report. Hashknife asked him if he had seen Jim Langley and Angel McCoy, but Sleepy hadn't. As far as he knew they had not been in town that morning.

About an hour later, Chuckwalla, Monty, and Steve came to town. They wanted to hear more about the shooting at Reimer's ranch, and Chuckwalla wanted to find out if Rance had any money in the bank to pay off the boys. It did not take long for Chuckwalla to find out that the bank did not give out any information, and they also told him that any money taken from the bank would have to be on a check signed by Rance McCoy himself.

Chuckwalla politely told Hale to go to hell, and left the bank bristling with anger. He explained the situation to Monty and Steve, who told him not to worry about them. Hashknife had talked with Slim, and had finally convinced Slim that Chuckwalla had nothing to do with the escape of Rance McCoy.

Hashknife found Butch Reimer in the Red Arrow, and asked Butch for a description of Kid Glover, which was willingly given. It tallied very well with the man Hashknife had seen.

"You ain't seen him, have yuh?" asked Butch anxiously.

"I think so, Reimer. Anyway, I saw a man of that description ridin' my gray horse."

"Why didn't yuh kill him?"

"Didn't think of it in time. I was wonderin' what he's doin' around here. After I find out, I'll probably have to kill him."

"Well, don't wait too long. I tell yuh, the man's a dirty snake."

"You didn't seem to think so the mornin' I first came to yore place, Reimer."

"Yeah, I did; but — well, he'd been with me a long time. Yuh see —" confidentially — "I had a quarrel with him, and I told him I'd kill him if he didn't leave the country. I can't tell yuh any more about it. I suppose his horse went lame; so he traded with yuh."

"And then came back to get yuh, eh?"

Butch's eyes shifted nervously.

"I'll be damned if I know, Hartley. But I'm scared he mistook Eddie Corby for me last night. I ain't got a bit of evidence ag'in' him — but somebody made a mistake. Corby never had an enemy around here. He never done anythin' to make an enemy."

"He must be pretty sore at yuh, Reimer."

"Well, I didn't know it was that bad. I'll sure keep my eyes open — and you better do the same. I told Slim just what I told you. Glover would kill yuh, if he thought yuh owned that gray horse. You take my advice — and shoot first."

"Well, I'm not goin' out to find him, if that's what yuh mean, Reimer."

Slim was interested in Hashknife's story of seeing Kid Glover. Merkle had been down to see him, demanding more action from the sheriff's office.

"I've either got to arrest somebody pretty soon, or I'll take a punch at Merkle and resign my office," declared Slim. "I don't even know where to start in. It's all mixed up."

Hashknife agreed with Slim. There did not seem to be anything to work on.

"Don'tcha know *anythin'?*" wailed Slim. "I admit that I ain't got no brains, Hashknife. The only thing I can think of doin' is to take a shot at everybody and then go on a long vacation. I'm gettin' jumpy, I tell yuh."

But Hashknife could offer no clues. He had a few theories of his own regarding things; but nothing for a sheriff to work on. Chuckwalla and his two men had left town about noon, and about two hours later Monty Adams rode back and came to the sheriff's office.

"Here's a funny deal," he told Slim. "While we was all in town this mornin', somebody got into the ranch-house and upset the whole place. I dunno what they was lookin' for, but they shore searched the old place. Even tore the blankets off the beds and smashed open an old trunk."

Slim shook his head wearily.

"Burglars, too, eh? By God, the next thing we know, we'll be havin' our pockets picked. What would anybody search the Circle Spade for?"

"That's what we'd like to know," replied Monty. "Chuckwalla thought yuh might like to know, Slim."

Hashknife grinned to himself, because he had seen Jim Langley and Angel McCoy going toward the Circle Spade. Were they expecting to find the hidden treasure in the ranch-house, he wondered? Did they think Rance McCoy had cached the loot from the Wells Fargo in his own house?

But as suddenly the inward grin departed. He seemed to hear Jim Langley saying:

"I'll bet yuh ten-to-one he never comes back."

Hashknife jerked out of his chair, swung out of the office, and headed for the Red Arrow, where he knew he would find Sleepy.

"What happened to the clam?" wondered Scotty McKay aloud. Scotty was still bandaged, but able to be about.

"Didja see him shoot out of here, Slim?"

Slim nodded wearily.

Hashknife started for the Red Arrow, but changed his mind and went to the post-office, where he inquired for mail. He knew there would be none, but he wanted a chance to converse with the postmaster, an old, gray-bearded man.

"You know Kid Glover, don'tcha?" asked Hashknife.

"Not very well," smiled the postmaster. "He seldom came in here."

"Didn't get much mail, did he?"

"Not much. He used to get a letter once in a while when he worked for Jim Langley."

"How long ago was that?"

"Oh, a year or so. Do you know him?"

"Never met him."

Hashknife went across to the Arrow, where he found Sleepy watching a poker game. Sleepy followed him outside and they went to the stable, where they saddled their horses. Sleepy asked no questions until they were a mile from town, traveling north along the JML road. Then —

"Where are we goin', Hashknife?"

"Jim Langley's ranch, Sleepy."

"Trouble?"

"Not unless somebody else starts it."

Neither of them had ever been at the JML, but they knew it was at the end of the road.

The JML was located on the bank of Lava Creek, near where it emptied into Red Arrow River; a two-story ranch-house, unpainted, one-story bunk-house, a stable bigger than the house, and numerous sheds and corrals. It was rather a picturesque old place, situated on an elevation which gave them a free view of the long sweep of hills to the south. To the east, only a short distance away, was the broken expanse of old lava beds.

Hashknife and Sleepy rode boldly up to the house and dismounted at the rickety front porch. There was no sign of life about the place until they walked around to the rear door, where they found Roper Briggs and "One-Eye" Connell, the JML cook. They were squatting on their heels near the kitchen door, but at sight of Hashknife and Sleepy, Briggs got quickly to his feet. He knew who Hashknife and Sleepy were, but did not speak until Hashknife smiled and nodded to both of them.

"How do yuh do," said Briggs drawlingly, and it seemed to Hashknife as though Briggs's eyes darted toward the open kitchen door.

"Just ridin' around," said Hashknife easily. "Where's Langley?"

"Dunno."

Briggs turned his head and looked toward the hills. One-Eye continued to glare with his remaining optic, but did not open his mouth. One-Eye was about sixty years of age, his sullen old jaws covered with a growth of gray bristles.

"Ain't home, eh?" queried Hashknife.

"He ain't," said Briggs flatly. "Whatcha want?"

"Nothin' much. We was ridin' up this way, so we thought we'd drop in and talk with Langley."

"All right; I'll tell him yuh called."

"That's fine of yuh. If yuh think he'll be back pretty soon, we'll wait for him, Briggs."

"Oh, hell, yuh can't tell when he'll be back. Might be pretty late."

"I see. You been here quite a while, ain't yuh?"

"Yuh mean, on the JML? Oh, about three year."

"You was workin' here while Kid Glover was here?"

"Shore was."

"Where'd he come from?"

"Montana, I reckon. Anyway, he talked about that State quite a lot."

"Railroaded up there," offered One-Eye. "Passenger brakeman. I used t' railroad on the G.N. I could have had an engine years ago if I'd stuck."

"He told yuh he used to be a passenger brake-man?" asked Hashknife.

"Shore. Me and him — say, whatcha want to know for?"

"I just wondered. I used to know a Glover over in the eastern part of the State, and I wondered if this was the same feller."

"I dunno; mebby was. I know he worked out of Missoula f'r a long time; so he said. I've been there."

"I heard he left the Half-Box R," said Briggs.

Hashknife nodded. Down in the nearest corral were three horses, and Hashknife could almost swear that two of them were the horses ridden that morning by Langley and Angel McCoy. Briggs glanced down that way and shot a quick glance at Hashknife, who was calmly taking his tobacco and papers from his pocket.

188

"Well, I suppose we might as well be goin', Sleepy," said Hashknife. "No use waitin' for Langley."

"No use, gents," agreed Briggs, visibly relieved. "He might be pretty late."

"McCoy with him?"

"Yeah."

"Well, much obliged, anyway. See yuh later."

Briggs walked around the house with them, and he was still there when Hashknife and Sleepy swung out of sight around a brushy curve on the road.

"Well, that didn't amount to much," said Sleepy.

Hashknife laughed softly.

"Mebby not; mebby yes. All depends."

"What put the idea into yore head to ask where that horse thief Glover came from?"

"Merely curious."

"I didn't even know Glover ever worked for the JML."

"Lotsa things you don't know, cowboy."

"You never knew a Glover in eastern Montana."

"I guess not, Sleepy."

"Oh, all right."

They rode back to Red Arrow and stabled their horses, after which Hashknife walked to the depot and sent a telegram to the Wells Fargo, asking for certain information on Paulsen, the messenger, who had been in charge of the express car the night of the robbery.

Slim had some news for Hashknife. Dell Blackwell and "Boomer" Weed had quit the Half-Box R. The murder of Ed Corby caused them to draw what they had coming, and they were now in Red Arrow. This left

189

only Einar Sorensen, a tall, colorless Swede, at the ranch with Butch.

"And I'll betcha Butch would like to quit, too," said Chuck Ring. "He's gettin' jumpy."

"Did the boys say anythin' about somebody gunnin' for 'em?" asked Hashknife.

"They didn't say," laughed Chuck. "But they wasn't takin' any chances. Somebody's gone crazy, I think."

"Looks thataway."

Later on in the day Hashknife told Slim about what he had seen in the hills that morning, describing the man as near as he could.

"That's Kid Glover all right," said Slim. "Why didn't yuh collect yore horse when yuh had a chance?"

"That would be the natural thing to do, Slim; but I'm the greatest person yuh ever seen to act unnatural. That black hat we found on the bridge that mornin' would just about fit Kid Glover."

"By God!" exploded Slim. He opened his safe and took out the black sombrero.

"That's where I've seen it!" he exclaimed. "Right on the head of Kid Glover! What do yuh know about that? Hashknife, do yuh suppose he had anythin' to do with the killin' of DuMond?"

"Looks as though he did."

"Well, I'll be damned! Let's go and get him."

"Why would he kill DuMond?"

"That don't matter. We've got his hat and —"

"Yeah, we've got the hat. But yuh can't hang a man for losin' a hat, can yuh? That don't prove anythin'."

190

"We'll get him for horse-stealin' and make him admit the rest of his crimes. Why, it might have been him who killed Corby!"

"Why would he kill Corby?"

"Mistook him for Butch Reimer."

"Why kill Butch Reimer?"

Slim shrugged his shoulders wearily. "You're the worst 'why' asker I ever knew."

"There's got to be reasons for everything, Slim. Men don't commit murder for the fun of it. Only a crazy man would kill without cause."

"Yeah, that's true. Why would he kill DuMond and Corby?"

"I can't answer that question — yet. And I'm afraid if we arrest Kid Glover for horse-stealin', we'll never know the answer. It's worth waitin' for, Slim."

"Do yuh think Glover ransacked the Circle Spade?"

"No."

"Then who did?"

"Remains to be seen, as the undertaker said when the hearse team ran away and smashed the casket. What would old Rance have in his house that anybody around here would want, Slim?"

"The express loot," quickly.

"Mebby you're right."

"But where's old Rance?"

"Don't ask me. Yuh goin' to be around here this evenin'?"

"Right here — why?"

"Oh, I might get an idea between now and dark, Slim. See yuh later. Oh, yeah; if there's a telegram comes to yuh — somethin' yuh don't know a thing about, just hang onto it, will yuh? I signed yore name to one I sent to-day."

"Sure, I will."

Hashknife found Sleepy at the Red Arrow with Chuck Ring, Scotty McKay, Dell Blackwell, and Boomer Weed. The two men from the Half-Box R had absorbed plenty of liquor, but were not parading their valor.

"I pulled out because I was scared," confessed Dell. "Mebby somebody mistook old Ed Corby for somebody else, but we don't know who that somebody else was. Me and old Boomer wasn't in what you'd call a dyin' mood; so we jist asked for our time. Yuh can't blame us, can yuh?"

"Prob'ly be a few hundred men killed around here before it's over," said Chuck. "Things like that kinda run in bunches. Eppy-demic, they call it."

Hashknife managed to get Dell Blackwell away from the rest of the crowd, and while Sleepy was trying to lead them in song, Hashknife asked Dell about the quarrel between Butch Reimer and Kid Glover.

"Quarrel?" Dell was slightly owl-eyed.

"Yeah — the reason Glover left the ranch."

"Uh-huh."

Blackwell scratched his nose thoughtfully.

"Reimer swore he'd kill Glover, yuh know," explained Hashknife. "And Glover high-tailed it out of the country."

"He did, eh?" Blackwell grinned foolishly. "First time I ever heard of it, Hartley. What did they quarrel over?"

"Butch didn't say."

"And he swore he'd kill Glover, eh? Sa-a-a-ay! Lemme tell yuh somethin', cowboy; Glover ain't scared of no man. I ain't got no use for him m'self; but I'm here to tell yuh, he's no runner. If Butch ever scared Kid Glover, he — a-a-aw, he never did!"

"All I know is what Butch told me."

"Don't believe him, Hartley; he was kiddin' yuh."

"Did Glover ever have any trouble with DuMond?"

"Na-a-a-aw! The only man DuMond ever had any trouble with was Rance McCoy. Old Rance shore made Billy show yaller. Let's have a drink."

"You know Glover used to be a railroad man, don'tcha?"

"Yeah; a brake-man. What'll yuh have?"

Hashknife had a drink with them and left the place. He had definitely established Glover as a former brakeman and Reimer as a liar. Ordinarily Hashknife would have paid no attention to the fact that Reimer had lied to him, but that he had lied about the reasons Glover had for leaving the Half-Box R made a lot of difference.

As he went back to the sheriff's office he saw Jim Langley and Angel McCoy riding in from the south end of the town. Langley waved at Hashknife, who returned the salute. They drew up at the Red Arrow hitch-rack and went in to the saloon.

Hashknife grinned at the two horses, which were not the same ones he had seen Langley and McCoy riding that morning, nor were they the ones he saw in the corral at the JML.

Slim was lying on a cot in the back of the office when Hashknife came in.

"Be all set to pull out as soon as it gets dark," said Hashknife softly. "We may find out somethin' tonight. I hope that telegram comes before we leave."

"I'd like to find out somethin'," agreed Slim wearily. "I had a visit from the county commissioners and the prosecutin' attorney today. They tell me I'm layin' down on the job. We shore said things to each other."

"That Wells Fargo man didn't stay long," observed Hashknife.

"Well, we had a prisoner. He said there wasn't anythin' for him to do as long as we thought we had the guilty man. Hashknife, the more I think about it, the more I'm of the opinion somebody ransacked the Circle Spade tryin' to find old Rance's cache.

"I don't blame 'em. My God, that's a lot of money. Just think of a hundred and thirty-two thousand in one grab! Who wouldn't try to get their hands on it? And that's why Kid Glover came back. He wanted to get a crack at it. But I'll bet old Rance is hidin' out, waitin' for a chance to grab the money and head out of the country.

"He'd know that a lot of folks would be lookin' for him, so he merely hides out until it kinda blows over. The Wells Fargo detectives are watchin' every exit to this Valley. He's got to be here. There ain't a place he can get out unless he flies out."

"What's yore opinion on all this killin', Slim?"

"Personal grudge. I think Rance McCoy killed DuMond. The more I think of it, the more certain I am. As far as Kid Glover's hat is concerned, I don't sabe it. I'm not even makin' a guess who shot Corby, except I think it was a mistake. They might have mistaken him for Butch. Dell Blackwell is no saint. Neither is Weed. It might have been either of them that Corby was mistaken for."

"That's all very fine," agreed Hashknife. "You think Kid Glover came back to try and find the money, eh? Then why is he hidin' out down there in the breaks?"

"He stole your horse, Hashknife."

"All right. Remember he was headin' away from this country so fast that he couldn't wait on a lame horse. Just at that time he grabbed the first horse he got his hands on. Would he care whose horse it was? He didn't know which way we were going. I'll bet he don't know yet whose horse he's ridin'. And yuh must remember he came back here, Slim. Kid Glover is down there in the breaks, hidin' out. He ain't hidin' out because he stole my horse."

"That's the worst of talkin' with you," sighed Slim. "I get an idea that I'm kinda proud about, and along you come and shoot it full of holes. Why don'tcha tell me a few, so I can argue yuh out of 'em?"

"I never express mine," grinned Hashknife. "At least, not until they're hole-proof. Suppose we go and eat? I'm shore hungry and it's almost dark."

Chuck and Sleepy were in front of the Red Arrow when Hashknife and Slim came out, and Chuck went over to take care of the office, while Sleepy followed the other two men up to the restaurant.

195

Chuck was standing in the doorway of the office when Butch Reimer and Sorensen rode in. Reimer reined his horse over to the sheriff's office, where he dismounted and came in where Chuck was lighting the lamp.

"Thought I'd stay in town tonight," said Butch. "Lost two of my hired men today, and I'm kinda leary over what has already happened."

"I don't blame yuh," grinned Chuck. "Set down. Things like that kinda make yuh jumpy. I know I'd be jumpy."

While they were talking a man came in, carrying a telegram, which he handed to Chuck.

"Thought yuh might want it," he said, laughing. "See if there's any answer."

Chuck opened the envelope and took out the telegram, which read:

PAULSEN WITH US EIGHTEEN MONTHS WAS WITH N. P. SEVERAL YEARS HAS GOOD RECORD WORKED OUT OF MISSOULA FOR YEAR.

WELLS FARGO EX. CO.

The telegram was addressed to the sheriff of Red Arrow. Chuck frowned over it. He hadn't the slightest idea what it was all about, so he told the telegraph operator that Slim would have to answer it himself.

When the operator left the office, Chuck showed the telegram to Butch Reimer.

"Paulsen?" said Butch seriously. "Who's he?"

196

"That was the name of the messenger who got held up in that train-robbery, Butch."

"Oh, yeah; I remember now. Where's Slim?"

"Eatin' supper with Hartley and Stevens."

"I reckon I'll eat, too."

Butch left the office, but he didn't go to the restaurant. At least he hadn't been there when the three men left. As soon as they got back to the office, Chuck gave Slim the telegram, who passed it on to Hashknife.

"That must be the answer to the one you sent," he said.

"That's the one," smiled Hashknife.

"Did Butch Reimer come over to the restaurant?" asked Chuck.

"Is he back in town?" queried Hashknife quickly.

"He is. Said he was too jumpy to stay on the ranch tonight. I thought he went over to the restaurant."

"Did he happen to be here when this telegram came?"

"Sure. The agent told me to read it and see if there would be an answer; so I did. But I didn't know what in hell it was all about."

"Did Butch read it?"

"Yeah. I didn't know it was anythin' —"

"It's all right," said Hashknife. "Just take a little run around, Chuck, and see if Butch is still here."

Chuck was back in ten minutes with the information that Butch Reimer, if he was still in town, was not visible.

"His horse is gone. Sorensen, Blackwell, and Weed are all over at the saloon, but there's no sign of Butch. And he ain't at the hotel."

Some one was coming along the sidewalk, and a moment later Jim Langley came in.

"What's new, Slim?" he asked. "Any news of old Rance?"

"Not a thing, Jim," replied Slim. "We're stuck."

"Pshaw. Me and Angel have been down in the country below the Half-Box R all day, so I thought I'd stop and see what was new."

He looked directly at Hashknife as he spoke to Slim, but Hashknife said nothing about being out at the JML that day.

"Somebody ransacked the Circle Spade ranch-house while the folks was all in town this mornin'," offered Chuck.

"The hell they did! What for, do yuh suppose?"

"Some enterprisin' person tryin' to find where Rance cached the loot," grinned Slim.

"Prob'ly. But do yuh still think Rance pulled that job?"

"Who else?"

"Well, that's the way I look at it."

"What does Angel think about it, Jim?"

"He don't say much. Well, we've got to be driftin', and it's a long ways home when you're tired. So-long, gents."

After Langley left the office, Hashknife wrote out a telegram, which he folded up and handed to Chuck Ring.

"Take that to the depot before yuh eat, Chuck. It's dark enough now, Slim. Saddle yore horse and meet us at the livery stable."

198

Slim hadn't the slightest idea where they were going, but he was willing to follow anybody who might help him make good on the job. Ten minutes later they met on the side street, and Hashknife led the way toward the Half-Box R. It was very dark, with no hint of a moon.

"That's our salvation," said Hashknife. "If it was moonlight, I'd never ride this road tonight. Travel fast and keep still. There'll be plenty of time to talk later on — if we're able."

It seemed a long way to the Half-Box R, riding blindly along the old dirt road, trusting to their mounts to keep the road. In single file they thundered across the bridge where Billy DuMond had lost his life, and the rather frail structure trembled under the thudding hoofs.

About a quarter of a mile from the ranch, as near as Hashknife could judge, they slowed to a walk.

"Got to be careful now," warned Hashknife. "Don't talk."

"I wish I knowed what it's all about," whispered Slim.

"Yuh won't know," replied Sleepy. "After it's all over, he'll tell yuh — and you'll wonder why yuh didn't think of it before."

"Don't talk," warned Hashknife.

Hashknife remembered that just before reaching the ranch-gate there was a culvert about four feet wide. As soon as they crossed it, he drew up his horse.

"You stay here, Sleepy," he said. "Block the road with yore horse, and don't let anybody get past yuh."

199

"Not anybody?" asked Sleepy.

"Not a dam' body!"

"Suits me fine. And you better talk nice when yuh come back, long-fellow. Good luck."

Hashknife and Slim disappeared in the darkness, leading their horses. Hashknife led the way around the fence and came in beside the corrals, where they tied their horses.

"Can yuh find the stable?" he whispered.

"Yeah," softly.

"Get down there, Slim. Mebby you'll find somebody's horse planted down there. Stop anybody that comes, even if yuh have to bend a gun over his head."

"Who will it be, Hashknife?"

"You take a chance on that. If yuh hear a shot at the house, you come runnin'."

Slim crawled through the corral fence and faded out in the night. From where Hashknife stood he could see the dark bulk of the ranch-house, with no lights showing. Slipping through the fence he cautiously made his way to the rear of the house, traveling almost as silently as a shadow in spite of his high-heeled boots. There was not a sound to be heard except the sleepy calling of a night-bird and the incessant chirp of a cricket.

Hashknife was not familiar with the interior of the ranch-house, but he remembered that there was a back porch, which was unusual in ranch-houses. He made his way silently around to the porch, slid in under the railing, and stood up against the back door, which was closed.

Hashknife felt sure that Butch Reimer had come back to the ranch, although there was no sign of him. It was so dark that objects were practically invisible at a few feet distance. The house was as still as a tomb. Cautiously he tested the door and found it unlocked. This was not at all unusual, as few doors in the cattle country were ever locked. Sneak thieves were unknown.

Hashknife's next move was a foolish one. He slowly opened the door, thrust his head and shoulders just inside the house and listened intently.

And it was then that his brain registered a soundless explosion; a burst of flame which gave off no sound — and for a time, at least, he lost all interest in anything that might happen at the Half-Box R.

Then he felt himself jerked back to consciousness, in which he was conscious of a heavy nausea and a throbbing pain in his head. He opened his eyes wearily and looked around. He was lying on the floor of a room, his head and shoulders propped against the wall, and on a box near him was an oil-lamp, turned low enough to make the other objects in the room indistinct.

His eyesight gradually cleared, and he saw a man, squatting on his heels a few feet away, looking at him intently. It was Kid Glover. His thin, dark features were sharply etched in the yellow lamplight, and his mop of black hair hung low over his forehead. In his right hand dangled a six-shooter, which Hashknife immediately recognized as his gun.

Hashknife sighed and closed his eyes.

"Don't play 'possum with me," growled Glover. "What in hell do you want here, feller?"

It was evident to Hashknife that Glover did not know him; which was fortunate for Hashknife. He opened his eyes and looked at Glover wearily.

"What do I want?" he said slowly. "I just stopped here, thinkin' I'd get a meal."

"Yeah?" Glover was not convinced. "Where you from?"

"Milk River, Montana."

"Yeah. Stranger, eh?"

"What happened to me?" queried Hashknife, feeling of his head and finding a swelling which compared favorably in size with a doorknob.

"You horned in where yuh wasn't wanted, feller."

"Evidently. Sorry to cause yuh all this trouble."

"No trouble." Glover grinned widely, and evidently with great satisfaction. "I jist popped yuh over the head and packed yuh up here."

He lifted a lariat rope off the floor and got to his feet.

"I'm goin' to tie yuh up for a while," he said. "You horned in on somethin' that don't concern yuh at all, so I'll jist fix yuh up with this string. Kinda want yuh to stay put for a while."

"Well, I'd rather be gettin' along," said Hashknife. "If you'd tell me where the nearest town is, I'd —"

"You ain't goin' to no town. And if you make any crooked move, I'll even up the two sides of yore head."

"Oh, I ain't goin' to do nothin'," assured Hashknife meekly. "I'm neutral."

"You better be."

Swiftly he roped Hashknife, who barely repressed a chuckle. There were many things that Kid Glover did not know about hog-tying a man. The slight bracing of a leg, an arm, an elbow, meant nothing to the Kid; but it meant that Hashknife could relax and almost slide out of the ropes.

Then he whipped out a dirty handkerchief, forced Hashknife's jaws open, and gagged him.

"I reckon you'll stay put," he said grimly. Then he blew out the light, crossed the floor, and Hashknife heard him going softly down the stair.

Relaxing his muscles Hashknife began releasing the ropes. It was ridiculously easy. He untied the gag, and stretched out on the floor. The exertion had caused his head to throb sickeningly. After a few minutes he began crawling to the head of the stairs. Just before he reached the stairs his hands came in contact with an old kitchen chair of considerable weight.

Downstairs a door closed softly, and in a few moments Hashknife saw the glow from a lamp. Came a sharp exclamation, silence; and then a harsh laugh.

"I thought you'd come back, you dirty sneak."

It was the voice of Kid Glover.

"Keep yore hands still, you dam' fool! That's the idea. Mebby yuh better unbuckle that belt. Just let it fall."

Came the thud of a belt and gun striking the floor.

"What do you want?" Butch Reimer's voice was not very steady.

"That's a hell of a question, you crooked pup."

"I never played crooked with you," denied Butch, hotly, it seemed. "By God, you tried to play crooked with me."

Kid Glover laughed mockingly.

"Yeah, and you knew I would, Butch. But I'm back now, and I'll take it all."

"The hell yuh will!"

"Yeah — the hell I will. You see if I don't. I told yuh I'd kill yuh if yuh ever played crooked with me, and I'm goin' to keep my word."

"You killed Billy DuMond."

"Did I? Try to prove it."

"And you killed Ed Corby."

"Thasso? I never had any trouble with that fool."

"You thought he was me."

Glover laughed sneeringly.

"Well," he said, "yuh know I'll keep my word. Now, where is the stuff?"

"You'll never know," he said defiantly.

"Won't I? Butch, you better tell me. I came to get it. You know me. I'll cut yore ears off if yuh don't talk."

"No, yuh won't, Kid. The only way you'll ever get anythin' out of it will be to throw in with me again. Laugh, if yuh want to. Why, you fool, everybody knows yuh came back. You traded horses with a man in Welcome, and you're still ridin' that horse. Know who owns that animal?"

"Aw, I don't give a damn who owns it."

"Don'tcha? Well, he's the slickest range detective in the West. He's been watchin' yuh, Kid. I seen a telegram to the sheriff today. By God, they've spotted

204

Paulsen! Don't ask me how they got wise. They'll get you, too. Me and you can pack up enough grub to carry us through, and we can cut out through the lava country. I've got the stuff, but you'll never know where it is. Go ahead and kill me if yuh think it'll save yore neck."

"How could they spot Paulsen? You're lyin', damn yuh! There ain't no way they can spot him. You're tryin' to get off cheap, Butch. I don't trust yuh, I tell yuh. What about this detective? How do yuh know he's been watchin' me?"

"Told me he was. Oh, he knows yuh. Why, he saw yuh with his horse, you ignorant fool. He's got you on the run right now."

"I'm not on any run. Who is he? What does he look like?"

Hashknife listened to Butch's description of him, and it was fairly accurate. When Butch finished, Kid Glover laughed chokingly.

"Butch, yuh may be right, at that. I've got to trust yuh a little, I suppose; but the first crooked move yuh make will be the last one yuh ever make. Lemme tell yuh somethin', Butch: yore wonderful detective is upstairs, roped tight and gagged tighter. He tried to sneak in on me a while ago, and I thought he was you; so I slammed him over the head with my gun and packed him upstairs. By God, he made me think he was a stranger. Ha, ha, ha, ha, ha!"

"You mean to tell me you've got —"

"I've got a man of that description, Butch."

"My God, that's luck! He was after me and you, Kid. What's our next move? If he's upstairs he can hear every word we say."

"What do we care," laughed Glover callously. "He ain't goin' nowhere. We'll shut his mouth pretty quick, and then we'll head for the lava beds."

"You mean — we'll bump him off, Kid?"

"Why not? You fool, it's him or us."

"Mebby he didn't come alone, Kid. He's workin' with Slim Caldwell, and Hartley's got a pardner. Better let me have my gun again. Two guns are better than one."

"I'll never be anythin' but a fool, I suppose," growled the Kid, and Hashknife guessed that Glover gave Butch his gun and belt.

"Better douse that light," said Butch. "We can light the lamp upstairs. Better wait until I fasten the doors. We don't want anybody sneakin' in on us right now."

Hashknife heard Butch working with the doors, and finally he came back to Glover.

Hashknife picked up the old chair, grasping it by the back, as he knelt close to the stairs. There was no railing around the stairway, and he saw the black bulk of the two men, as their head and shoulders came above the floor-level.

The next instant the heavy chair crashed down upon them, swung with every ounce of strength in Hashknife's arms and shoulders. Rungs splintered out of it, and Hashknife swayed sharply sideways to keep from falling down on them, when his hands held nothing but the back of the chair.

He heard a sharp grunt, the bumping crash of a falling body, a wondering curse, and then he flung himself over the edge of the stairway, landing on a yielding bulk, which he knew was the body of one of the men.

As he reached frantically down, searching for the man's holster, his hand came in contact with a revolver, lying on a step. Swiftly he sprang down the remaining steps and into the front room of the ranch-house just as the front door was jerked open.

Hashknife fired one shot, but he was sure it missed. The man had darted to the right, and Hashknife ran through the doorway after him, vaulting the railing, running halfway to the rear of the house, where he paused to listen.

"Hashknife!" called Slim's voice softly from toward the stable.

"Up here," replied Hashknife, and in a moment Slim had joined him. Hashknife was thankful that Slim did not ask questions.

"I got yore gray horse and another one," he whispered. "The gray was behind the stable, so I moved it away. Then a man rode in and tied to the corral. I kept down, and as soon as he left the horse, I swiped it."

"Good boy! Where did that feller go, Slim?"

"I heard him runnin', and I think he went around the house."

"Around the house, eh? By golly, I bet he went back in. Look out for him, Slim."

They sneaked back to the front porch and found the door closed. Hashknife knew it was wide open when he came out and there had been no breeze to close it.

Suddenly came the sound of a muffled shot inside the house.

"Get to the back door!" said Hashknife.

Slim raced around the house, while Hashknife sprang to the porch and flattened himself against the wall beside the door. He heard somebody in the house. It sounded as though somebody had struck a piece of furniture. Then he heard heavy footsteps near the door.

Hashknife gripped his gun tightly and swung up his hand as the door opened and a man surged out. But Hashknife did not strike him. Instead, he dived forward, wrapping his long, muscular arms around the man, and together they plunged off the few steps to the ground.

The man did not offer any resistance. In fact, it was as though Hashknife had tackled a dummy. Quickly he twisted the man's right arm behind his back, holding him down with his knees, and called to Slim, who came on the run.

"Hold this whipperwill," said Hashknife. "I think he's all raveled out, but yuh never can tell."

They exchanged places and Hashknife went into the house. Moving slowly back to the stairway, he halted at the sound of a groan and scratched a match.

Lying near the foot of the stairs was Butch Reimer, flat on his face, arms outspread. As quickly as possible Hashknife lighted the lamp and called to Slim, who came in, carrying the limp form of Kid Glover.

Hashknife turned Butch over. The bullet had struck him over the right eye, knocking away a generous chunk of his head, and from there it cut a nasty-looking furrow along the side of the head to a point just above his ear. He was bleeding freely, and while the shock had knocked him out, there was nothing serious about it.

Kid Glover was a sight. As far as Hashknife could determine, the Kid had borne the brunt of the heavy chair. But he had evidently recovered sufficiently to shoot Butch and to stagger outside, trying to get away.

CHAPTER
NINETEEN

Part of the Truth

Hashknife stood up from his examination and grinned at Slim, who didn't know yet what it was all about.

"Where does Butch figure in this?" he asked. "Was the tryin' to protect Glover?"

They turned at a sound and saw Sleepy at the doorway, gun in hand.

"I heard some shootin'," he said simply, and came in to look at Butch and the Kid.

"I crowned the Kid with a chair," said Hashknife. "He got me first. Knocked me down and tied me up, but he don't know much about ropes. Then him and Butch decided to throw in together, put me out of my misery and clear out; but I got loose and smashed a chair on the Kid's head. I think Butch decided to get back in the house and recover his gun, and the Kid shot him in the dark, not knowin' who he was."

The Kid blinked his eyes and sat up, rubbing his head. He squinted painfully at Hashknife, shifted his eyes to Slim and Sleepy, and then looked at Butch. The Kid was not shamming — he was very sick.

"You shot Butch," said Hashknife.

The Kid grimaced painfully at Hashknife.

"I guess I didn't tie yuh very tight," he said.

"Not tight enough, Glover. Butch ain't hurt much, and as soon as he recovers I think he'll tell where the plunder is cached."

"What plunder?"

"The stuff you came back to get. You tried to play crooked with Reimer and DuMond, didn't yuh? But they shifted the cache and left a dummy package for you to skip away with. Oh, I've got you cinched, Glover. By this time the Wells Fargo have arrested Paulsen. You was a brake-man on the same train that Paulsen worked on in Montana.

"You framed it with Paulsen, you and Butch and DuMond. It was a cinch. Paulsen opened the door and let Reimer in. You broke the train in two at Curlew Spur, Reimer pulled the job lone-handed, while DuMond handled the horses. Oh, we've got yuh where the hair is short."

"Prove it," snarled the Kid. "You can't, damn yuh!"

Butch was beginning to make funny noises and trying to sit up. Hashknife nudged Sleepy and whispered:

"Take Glover into the kitchen, Sleepy. Watch the little snake. Slim will light a lamp for yuh."

They went away with Glover, while Hashknife squatted on his heels, watching Butch fight his way back to consciousness. Butch had lost considerable blood, and the shock of the heavy bullet had dazed him badly. But he finally opened his eyes, and gradually a look of understanding overspread his face. His right

211

hand, hanging limp at his side, twisted over against his empty holster.

Slim came back to the front room and Butch scowled at him.

"The Kid shot yuh, Butch," said Hashknife.

Butch started to speak, but changed his mind.

"Oh, we've got him," assured Hashknife. "He hasn't done anything but talk since we tied him up. He seemed to think we'd turn him loose if he spilled the whole plot, but he's such a liar that we don't believe him."

"What's he say?" groaned Butch.

"He said it was you and DuMond that framed the scheme with Paulsen. I think he lied, myself, because him and this crooked messenger used to work together. He said he merely introduced Paulsen to you, and that —"

"He's a dirty liar!" snarled Butch.

"We thought so," said Hashknife seriously. "And then he told us that you killed DuMond, in order to increase yore size of the pot."

Butch raised himself up on one elbow.

"Where is that dirty liar?" he demanded hoarsely. "By God, he killed Billy himself. He came back here to kill me, too. He's a sneakin' little crook. He raided the cache and tried to get away with it all, I tell yuh. We knowed he'd do it; so we made up a dummy bundle. That's how he happened to cripple his horse, gettin' away fast — and that's why he traded horses with yuh."

"I felt that for a long time, Butch. And he killed Corby, didn't he?"

"Sure as hell, he did! He thought he could kill me and find the cache. None of the rest of my boys know anythin' about it. Bring in that dirty little sidewinder and I'll make him eat every word he said about me."

"That was his hat we found on the bridge, Butch."

"I knew it. I was scared you'd work somethin' out of it."

"It sure helped," grinned Hashknife. "And another thing, Reimer. The night of that holdup, which one of yuh knocked old Rance McCoy down and robbed him?"

"DuMond," said Butch readily. "He hated the old man. Billy saw a chance to get him right. He wanted to kill McCoy, and thought he did, but I reckon it was a glancin' blow."

"And was it DuMond's idea to take McCoy's horse down there where yuh held up the train and shoot it?"

"Yeah — his and Glover's. Glover mentioned it, and the Kid carried it out. He shot the horse before we went to Curlew Springs."

"Whose idea was it to skin out the brand?" asked Slim.

"I dunno. The Kid and Billy saw you and yore two men ride out there that mornin', and then they trailed yuh over to the Circle Spade, to see if yuh arrested Rance. After yuh left there and headed back for town, Billy said they got the idea of skinnin' out the brand and stealin' the saddle — tryin' to make it look worse for Rance."

"I thought that was the way of it."

"But how did you know it wasn't a bullet from the car that killed the horse?"

"That was a cinch. The cut is pretty deep there, Reimer, and any bullet fired from the car door at a horse outside the right-of-way fence would naturally range upward. The bullet that killed the horse was fired from slightly above the animal, ranging downward. And what holdup man would ever leave his horse in full view of the train?"

Butch rubbed his sore head and groaned a few times.

"That's the hell of makin' it too strong," he said.

Hashknife walked to the kitchen door, opened it, and said to Sleepy:

"Bring in yore company."

The Kid and Butch glared at each other.

"Butch says you're a liar," grinned Hashknife.

"The hell I am! What about?"

"He says it was you that framed the deal with Paulsen."

The Kid started toward Butch, but Sleepy yanked him back.

"And you know damn well it's the truth!" rasped Butch.

"You fool!" screamed the Kid, trying to tear loose from Sleepy. "What have you told?"

"Told?" queried Butch blankly. "Why, you told 'em —"

"Oh, you poor fool! I never told anythin'!"

Butch slumped back on the floor, glaring his hate at Hashknife, who grinned over his cigarette.

214

"Try and find the money!" snarled Butch. "By God, you'll never find it."

"No?" Hashknife looked pityingly at Butch. "Listen to me, pardner. You're close to fifty, ain't yuh? They'll give yuh close to twenty-five years for this job. Twenty-five years in the penitentiary is a long time. You'll be an awful old man when yuh come out. The money won't help yuh none. Mebby we can find it ourselves. But if yuh give it all up and tell the prosecutor the truth about the whole deal, yuh might cut that sentence down to where you'll still be worth killin' when yuh get out."

Butch laughed harshly, shaking his head.

"What would I get off?" asked Glover.

"They'd only hang you once."

"That's a hell of a lot."

"You ought to be hung once a week," growled Butch. Then he sobered suddenly and looked at Slim.

"I've got to have more than the word of that Hashknife bloodhound, Slim."

"I can't promise anythin'," said Slim. "You'll have to make yore deal with Merkle."

Slim went after the horses, and came back leading three. The tall gray horse nuzzled Hashknife violently, and acted as if he'd found a long-lost friend.

"Damn that horse!" snorted Kid Glover. "If I'd left it alone, everythin' would have been all right."

"If you hadn't been born a horse-thief, we'd have been all right, yuh mean," retorted Butch.

They roped the two prisoners to their horses and started back to Red Arrow. There were three aching heads, a jubilant sheriff, and one sour cowboy — the latter being Sleepy, who had shared in none of the action.

"You'll get into it," assured Hashknife.

"Yea-a-ah — next time! Next time, you watch yore own back trail. I spend a week or so watchin' you build up to a big climax, and then don't even shoot off a roamin' — candle."

"I swear, I can't hardly realize it yet," declared Slim. "I heard yuh tell it all, Hashknife. Oh, I don't get any of the credit. I didn't know what was goin' on half the time."

"Yuh never will — around him," complained Sleepy.

"Well, he'll get that five thousand," said Slim.

"And give it to some orphin' asylum, prob'ly."

"Five thousand!" snorted Glover. "Why didn't yuh throw in with us, Hartley?"

"You made me mad when yuh stole my horse."

CHAPTER
TWENTY

Fire

Angel McCoy did not ride back to the JML with Langley that evening. He had a few drinks at the Red Arrow and decided to stay a while. Langley tried to argue him into going back to the ranch, but Angel was stubborn. Whiskey usually affected him that way, so Langley rode on alone.

Sorensen, Blackwell, and Weed were trying to spend the money they had drawn from Reimer, and with them Angel found congenial companionship. They were deliberately getting drunk. Angel was able to drink a lot of whiskey and still not show it in his actions, but his talk usually gave him away. He became rabid, devilish; an anarchist without a bomb. Even the other cowboys wished that Angel would hang up his gun before he began drinking.

"Where's that sheriff?" he demanded, after the rest of the boys had grown goggle-eyed. "He's the whipperwill I'm layin' for."

"What did Slim ever do to you?" asked the bartender.

"Hit me," snarled Angel. His pale face looked yellow in the lamplight, like old ivory, and his eyes glistened.

217

"Hidju?" queried Boomer Weed. "Whaffor?"

"None of yore business!"

"Hidju hard?"

"I told yuh to shut up, didn't I?"

"Didee, Dell? Didee tell me to shud'p?"

Dell Blackwell nodded solemnly.

"I heard'm menshun't," said Dell. "'S far's that's consherned, I trail m' bets with Slim. F'r money, marbles, 'r chalk, he c'n whip yuh on a sheepskin, Angel."

"He couldn't whip me no time," declared Angel.

"Le's go fin' him," suggested Boomer. "Might's well have more fight'n lesh talk. Whatcha shay, Angel? No, don't make fashes at me, Angel. Ha, ha, ha, ha, ha! You're shore, yuh pale-fashed card-sharp. Slim swiped yore girl."

Angel flushed crimson and his hand streaked for his gun, but Blackwell was still sober enough to clinch with him and prevent him from drawing the gun.

"Let 'm loosh," coaxed Weed. "I c'n han'le him, Dell."

"You ought to keep yore mouth shut," said the bartender. "Don't start no gun-battles in here."

"Ho, ho, ho, ho, ho!" roared Sorensen with a sudden excess of mirth. "Anchel vant somebody to holt him. He don't try git loose."

"You dam' Swede!" snarled Angel impotently.

"Led him loose," said Sorensen. "I squirsh him."

"You fools calm down," growled the bartender. "This ain't no place to start fights."

"You hang onto yourself, Angel," warned Dell. "Weed's drunk. Don't start no gun-play; sabe?"

Angel shook out his twisted sleeve, glaring at Weed, who laughed owlishly at him and offered to buy a drink.

"Damn you and yore drinks!" snapped Angel.

Chuck Ring came sauntering in, and Boomer immediately got hold of his belt.

"C'mon and have a drink, Chuck. I jus' had a battle with Angel. He says he's goin' to crawl Slim Caldwell."

"Thasso?" Chuck looked curiously at Angel, who stood apart from them, glaring at Boomer.

"What you got ag'in' old Slim, McCoy?" asked Ring.

"That's my business."

"Yea-a-ah? And yuh aim to git him, eh?"

"Well?" defiantly.

"Not so dam' well," said Chuck dryly. "You monkey with Slim and you'll think the seat of yore pants got caught in the door of a volcano. Lemme tell yuh a few things, Angel. You start anythin' round here and they'll take you up on a broom. You're a bad actor in yore own mind. You may be able to hang the Injun-sign on old Rance McCoy, but to us, you're just another dirty shirt that needs doin' up. Yuh play a crooked game, pardner — and that lets yuh out. Now, yuh better trot along home and forget all that talk about 'gettin'' Slim Caldwell. I know why yuh hate Slim. Everybody in town knows it, Lila as well, and it won't do yuh no good with her. If I was in yore boots, I'd cut me a straight trail out of this country and not leave a single blaze."

Angel's face was colorless now, even to his lips, which were a white line across his white face, and his eyes were half-closed, twitching at the outer corners. But he made no move to resent what Chuck had said. Angel was fast with a gun, but he knew Chuck was as fast. And there were three more guns to account to — not counting the one behind the bar, in easy reach of the bartender.

For at least ten seconds he stood there immovable, before he stepped up to the bar a few feet away from Weed, and asked for whiskey. There was nothing of the craven about Angel. He drank alone, keeping one hand on the bottle.

"Don't be a fool," cautioned the bartender.

"I'm payin' for what I get," replied Angel evenly.

"Embalmin' his guts," said Blackwell. "Lotsa folks have to do that to keep their nerve."

But Angel did not even look toward Blackwell. As far as appearances went, he might have been an entire stranger enjoying a few drinks alone. But Chuck watched him. He knew Angel was steeping his soul in liquor, either trying to deaden the sting of what Chuck had said or to brew a fresh devil in his mind.

Chuck had no mean capacity himself, but he was human enough to get drunk in a reasonable length of time. He counted Angel's drinks in the next half-hour, and the total was twelve. Twelve drinks of raw whiskey on top of what he had already taken.

And all the effect it had was to cause Angel's lips to draw back in a sneering grin, as he looked at himself in the back-bar mirror. Nor did his hand tremble as he filled the twelfth glass to the top.

Then he walked steadily to the door, where he turned and looked coldly at the group in front of the bar. All except Chuck were owl-eyed with liquor. Chuck watched him closely, anxiously. But all Angel did was to throw back his head and laugh hollowly at them, as though defying them to harm him in any way. Then he stepped outside and went up the street.

Chuck surged away from the bar, swearing softly, and went to the front door, where he saw Angel go down the street, walking as straight as though he had not taken a drink. He stopped in front of Parker's store, where he seemed to be looking through the window, after which he turned and came back to the Eagle hitch-rack, where he mounted his horse and rode out of town, heading toward the JML ranch.

Chuck sighed with relief as he saw Angel ride away. He did not want trouble with Angel, but he realized that it would be inevitable if Angel stayed in Red Arrow. Blackwell, Sorensen, and Weed were past even the humorous stage now; so Chuck deposited them in convenient chairs, where they might slumber until closing time.

"Where'd Angel go, Chuck?" asked the bartender.

"Home."

"That's good. He's the craziest puncher I ever knew. But can't he pack liquor! Mister man, he's the hollowest human I ever knowed. Have a drink, Chuck?"

"I hope to die if I do. One more drink and the dignity of my office is all shot to hell. Good-night."

Chuck went back to the office, where Scotty was playing solitaire, and told Scotty about Angel.

"I wouldn't tr-rust him as far as I could throw a fr-reight wagon," declared Scotty, shoving the cards aside. "He has the same glint in his eye that ye see in the eye of an outlaw cayuse. Now, where do ye suppose Slim and the two boys have gone, Chuck?"

"Slim didn't know," laughed Chuck. "He follows Hashknife around like a good old pup, with Sleepy trailin' both of 'em. But Hashknife's no fool."

"Not a bit o' one," agreed Scotty earnestly. "I'd hate to be in Kid Glover's boots when that tall cowpuncher meets up with him. Didja ever study the length of Hartley, takin' account of the way his muscles work? They're long, like the muscles in a snake. But he's —"

From far up the street came a wailing cry. It was repeated several times before Chuck and Scotty reached the door. It was a woman's voice they heard, crying —

"Fire! Fire! Fire!"

"Fire!" snorted Chuck, stepping out on the sidewalk. There were people running from Parker's store, and more from other places of business. Chuck and Scotty ran up the street and crossed over to the crowd. The woman was Mrs. Parker.

"It's the Parker home!" yelled one of the men. "Get some buckets!"

Chuck raced back to the office, where he secured a large bucket and an axe. As he came through the doorway, Hashknife, Sleepy, Slim, and their two prisoners rode up to the front of the office.

222

"Parker's house is on fire!" yelled Chuck, paying no attention to the prisoners, as he raced up the street.

"I'll hold 'em," said Sleepy. "Go ahead."

Hashknife and Slim threw the lead-ropes to Sleepy, and went galloping toward the Parker home, passing the scattered crowd and jerking to a stop at the gate, where they dismounted and ran toward the house.

As yet the fire was confined to the front of the house, but blazing merrily. The door was open and the flames were billowing out, fanned by a breeze from the rear. The crowd came piling in, knocking down the picket-fence.

They headed for the well at the rear of the house, led by Jim Parker. Slim grabbed him by the arm, forcing him to stop.

"Where's Lila?" demanded Slim.

"God knows!" panted Parker. "She was at home alone. My wife was at the store, and when she came home the house was on fire."

Slim and Hashknife ran to the back door, dashing through the smoke and found the stairway. Slim pushed Hashknife aside and leaped up the stairs. Hashknife managed to close the door between the hall and the living-room, but not until he had caught a fairly good view of the blazing interior. He caught a glimpse of the center-table, lying on its side, and almost in the center of the room on the floor was the big lamp, which usually sat on the table.

Almost before Hashknife had closed the door, fighting against the smoke-fumes, Slim was staggering down the stair. Together they stumbled out of the house and into the cool night air, where they panted like a pair of Marathon runners. Men were running back and forth from the well, tossing ineffectual buckets of water through the windows, while others shouted advice, which nobody heeded.

"She's not up there," panted Slim. "I was in every room."

Everybody in Red Arrow was there, it seemed, and the word had been passed that Lila was in the house. Mrs. Parker was crying, Jim Parker swearing.

Hashknife drew Parker aside.

"Any idea how it happened, Parker?"

"Hell, no!"

"Lila ain't in there. Me and Slim searched."

"Thank God for that, Hartley!"

Parker ran back to tell the women. The house was doomed, and everybody seemed to realize it. Hashknife and Slim drew back nearer the fence when the flames shot through the roof with a crackle like a machine gun. Chuck, sweating, his shirt on fire in several places, came to them.

"Whatsa use?" he asked. "Yuh can't do a thing, Slim."

"Not a thing, Chuck. How did it get started?"

"Nobody knows. Ain't she a dinger of a fire, though? Look at her blaze!"

Dell Blackwell and Boomer Weed, still half-drunk, joined them. They had tried to carry buckets of water, but neither of them could find the well after the first trip.

"What became of Angel?" asked Slim.

"He went home," said Chuck. "I shore told him where to head in at, didn't I?"

"If I remember right, yuh did," agreed Blackwell dryly.

"How long ago did he go home?" asked Slim quickly.

"Fifteen or twenty minutes ago," replied Chuck. "Mebby it was a little longer, but I don't think so."

"C'mon, Hashknife!" snapped Slim. "You, too, Chuck! Never mind the fire — c'mon!"

Slim led them back at a brisk trot. Scotty saw them going away, and followed after.

"What's the matter?" asked Chuck.

"Don't ask me now," replied Slim. "Wait and see."

CHAPTER
TWENTY-ONE

The Finish at the JML

"What didja find out, Jim?"

Jim Langley helped himself to a generous cut of beef and leaned aside to let One-Eye Connell pour him a cup of coffee.

"Didn't find out a thing, Jess."

"Yuh seen Hartley, yuh say?" queried Jess Fohl.

"Yeah, I saw him. One-Eye, this coffee is cold."

"Yuh didn't give me time to heat her, Jim. We had supper two hours ago. You didn't say when you'd come back."

"Heat the stuff up a little, will yuh?"

"What did Hartley want yuh for, Jim?" asked Briggs.

"Not a thing! I think you and One-Eye are loco."

"Like hell!" snorted Briggs. "Leave it to One-Eye if he didn't say he came to see yuh. He even wanted to wait for yuh. Ain't that right, One-Eye?"

"Gospel truth, Jim."

"Well, he didn't say a word to me about bein' here."

"That's what looks funny to me," said Briggs. "He's no fool, Jim. Are you goin' to ignore everythin' Slim told yuh about him?"

Langley swallowed a mouthful of food, blinking thoughtfully.

"He's got nothin' on us, Boomer," said Langley.

"Yuh don't know a thing about him. Angel stayed in town, didn't he? Drinkin'?"

"That's his business; he's of age, Boomer."

"And with the brain of a five-year-old savage. He'll get drunk and pull a fight with somebody. He's sore at Slim Caldwell over that girl business. You know him well enough to sock him over the head and bring him out here roped on a bronc. By God, I've had about enough of him myself, Jim. He ain't quite human, if yuh ask me about him."

"If you're scared, why don't yuh quit?" asked Langley.

"The road is wide open, Roper."

"I'm no quitter, Jim," he said quickly. "Neither am I a fool. My neck is worth more to me than most anythin' I've got, and I don't like to have a crazy fool riskin' it for me."

Langley shoved back his plate impatiently.

"Write yore own ticket, Boomer," he said wearily. "I'm tired of hearin' yuh complain. Let's have a round of poker."

"Here or in the bunk-house?" asked Fohl.

"Here."

One-Eye cleared off the table, wiped up the crumbs, and stacked the dishes in a pan, while Langley produced the chip-rack and the cards.

"Yuh got to stand me off for a few dollars," said Jess Fohl. "I'm plumb busted, Jim."

Roper Briggs walked through the front room and out to the front porch. It was very dark, but he could see a dull glow in the direction of Red Arrow. He watched it several moments, and then came back into the house, where he picked up Langley's field-glasses.

"There's a fire in Red Arrow," he called to the boys, and went out on the porch.

They followed him out. It was rather hard to tell just where the fire was. It seemed much closer than Red Arrow.

"Must be in town," said Langley. "No house or hay-stack between here and Red Arrow."

"Jist enough wind to burn the town," said Fohl.

"Well, we can't help it," said Langley. "Let's play cards."

They went back and started their game, but there was an undercurrent of nervousness which caused them to play in a forced, jerky manner. Briggs continually listened, and he soon had the others doing the same thing.

"Aw, hell!" snorted Langley. "This makes me tired. What are you listenin' for, Roper?"

"I dunno," confessed Roper foolishly. "What's the rest of yuh listenin' for? I'm not doin' it alone."

"Well, quit it! Yuh make me jumpy. Gimme three cards, One-Eye. Three cards! My God, can'tcha count? Not five — three!"

"Don't bark at me!" roared One-Eye, who was usually rather soft-spoken.

"You've got it, too, have yuh?" Langley threw his cards down on the table and shoved his chair back.

228

"What's that?" exclaimed Roper Briggs.

It was the sound of a running horse which stopped down by the corral. Roper stepped to the door and flung it open, while the others crowded in behind him. They could hear a voice swearing — Angel McCoy's voice.

Jim Langley shoved the other men aside and went striding down to the corral, followed by the others. It was so dark they could not see Angel and his horse until they were close to him. He was laughing drunkenly.

"What is wrong with you, Angel?" demanded Langley.

"Wrong with me?" Angel laughed drunkenly. "Nothin' wrong with me. But I made that town set up and notice. They'll remember me, damn their dirty skins! Whoa, Sally Ann!"

"Who have you got there?" snapped Langley. "A-a woman! Angel, you fool! What have you done now?"

"My woman!" rasped Angel. "Git away from her, Langley!"

"A woman?" gasped Briggs.

"His woman?" wondered Fohl. "Why, the fool ain't —"

Langley scratched a match, shielding it from the breeze. Angel was backed against his horse, one arm flung around Lila, the other hand holding a cocked six-shooter. Lila's face was bloodless, her waist torn, a sleeve fluttering in the wind. Then the match went out.

"Oh, you fool!" wailed Briggs. "You awful fool!"

"Angel" — Langley's voice shook with emotion — "Angel, have a little sense. My God, don'tcha know what you've done? C'mon in the house."

"What have I done?" Angel's voice was querulous. "I'm my own boss, ain't I? They gave me the worst of it, and I'm payin' 'em back. And I'm payin' Slim Caldwell, damn his dirty heart. Don't touch me, Langley — none of yuh."

"Come in the house," begged Langley. "Mebby we can git things straight."

"I'll come in, Langley; but don't touch us. Go ahead — we'll come."

The men of the JML went ahead and entered the lighted kitchen, while close behind them came Angel and Lila. He had her right hand gripped at the wrist, and was still carrying his cocked gun. He shoved her in ahead of him, and stood there, glaring at them. He was hatless, and there were marks on his face which showed that Lila had not come willingly. She was panting heavily, and Langley thought she was going to faint, but when he started to get her a chair, Angel threw up his gun.

"Stay where yuh are, Langley," he said harshly.

"Sure," agreed Langley.

"Oh, let me go," begged Lila.

Angel laughed mockingly.

"The — the house was on fire," panted Lila. "We — we upset the table and the lamp fell."

"So that's what the fire was, eh?" muttered Briggs. "We could see it from here."

230

"Nice little blaze, eh?" laughed Angel. "Oh, they'll all remember me. I paid him back, the greaser. Ha, ha, ha, ha, ha, ha! This is good!"

"And they'll hang you so damned high —!" exclaimed Briggs.

"Hang me? I wasn't born to be hung, Roper."

"But don't yuh realize what this will mean?" asked Langley. "They'll know you took her, Angel."

"How will they? Nobody seen me. They'll think she burned in the fire. Oh, I was sure she was alone. I seen Mrs. Parker in the store. That house was half-burned before anybody discovered it, I'll bet."

Langley shrugged his shoulders helplessly.

"Go and take her back, Angel. Sneak around and leave her in town. If they come here after you, it'll give yuh a chance to make a getaway."

"The hell yuh say! Give her up? You must think I'm crazy."

"You can't keep her here, Angel."

"I didn't intend to. Give her up? Why, you damned fool, it took me a long time to get her this far. I didn't know a woman could fight so hard."

"But where can yuh take her, Angel? You'll never get her out of this Valley."

"Won't I? Once I get into the lava beds, all hell won't stop me."

"You crazy fool!" grunted Briggs. "You haven't a —"

Briggs had been standing with his arms folded, but now he dropped his hands, and perhaps Angel thought he was going to draw a gun. At any rate, Angel's wrist crooked and the report of his revolver shot shook the

231

room. Briggs jerked sideways, falling into Fohl, who tried to save him, and almost fell with him.

"Good God!" exclaimed Langley.

Angel was crouched forward, his gun held tensely in his hand. Lila swayed against the wall, her eyes wide with the horror of what she had seen.

"Keep away from me," warned Angel. "Nobody can stop me, I tell yuh. Keep yore hands where they are. By God, I'll kill anybody who tries to stop me."

"Nobody goin' to stop yuh, Angel," said Langley. "Don't shoot any more. We'll help yuh get away."

"There's somebody comin'!" exclaimed Fohl. "Hear 'em?"

Angel released Lila in order to swing the door shut with a kick of his elbow.

"The lamp!" whispered Fohl. "They can see through a window."

With a single stride Angel reached the table and blew out the lamp. "Keep away from me," he warned. "Don't touch me, damn yuh!"

"Shut up, you fool!" hissed Fohl, bold in the darkness. "Lila, if you're wise, get down on the floor."

"Stay where yuh are, Lila," commanded Angel.

Except for their labored breathing, there was no sound in the room. Langley had moved into the front room, and was trying to see through the front windows.

"I heard several horses," whispered Fohl.

"Shut up!" hissed Angel.

". . . the brain of a five-year-old savage," muttered a voice. It was Roper Briggs, talking in a delirium.

232

"I'm no quitter," he said distinctly. ". . . neck's worth more to me — my God, I'm thirsty! Whatcha drinkin', Jim?"

"Make that fool shut up!" rasped Angel.

"He's out of his head," whispered Fohl.

". . . put all our necks in a noose," babbled Briggs.

"Choke that fool!"

"Choke him yourself — you shot him."

"Water," begged Roper.

"Can't I get him some water?" asked Lila.

"Stay where yuh are," ordered Angel.

"Can yuh see anythin' from there, Jim?" whispered One-Eye.

"Not a damn thing. Are yuh sure yuh heard any —"

Some one was knocking on the front door.

"Come out, Langley."

It was Slim Caldwell's voice, hoarse with emotion.

"Sh-h-h-h!" warned Angel.

"Don't play 'possum," warned Slim. "The place is surrounded. We found Angel McCoy's horse, and we know he's in there. Bring him out, Jim. And another thing; if that girl is harmed, we'll hang every damned one of yuh."

"Yuh see!" whispered Fohl bitterly. "They've got all of us, Angel. Damn yore skin, I'd like to kill you."

"Let me go out," begged Lila.

Angel laughed softly. He still had her wrist.

Roper Briggs was trying to sing.

". . . for I'm a poo-o-o-or cowboy and I know I've done wrong. Beat the drum slowly and play the fi-i-ife

233

slowly; play the dead march as you bear me alo-o-o-ong."

"Roper, for God's sake, don't sing that," begged Fohl.

"Kick him in the head," said Angel callously.

"You try it!" snapped Fohl. "If I knowed just where you was —"

"Are yuh comin' out, Langley?" asked Slim Caldwell.

"No, damn yuh!" roared Langley. "If yuh want me, come and get me."

"And that finishes everythin'," wailed One-Eye.

Angel laughed with evident pleasure.

"Laugh, you crazy devil!" gritted Fohl.

"It's a fifty-fifty bet," said Langley. "We won't go out and they don't dare come in."

"Ninety-ten," corrected One-Eye. "We'll have to come out sooner or later."

"You yaller old quitter," sneered Angel. "We'll show 'em a trick or two, Jim."

"Take the girl upstairs," said Langley. "There's no use in her gettin' shot up."

"She goes where I go," declared Angel. "Whither thou goest, I will go, eh, Lila? Ha, ha, ha, ha, ha! All my life I've wanted to fight against odds, and now I've got a chance."

"You crazy fool," wailed Fohl. "Why didn't yuh pick yore odds a long ways from here?"

"Quit, if yuh want to, Jess," said Langley. "Walk right out and give up. They might pad the rope for yuh."

"Aw, they can't hang us," said One-Eye hopefully.

234

"They can hang Angel," said Fohl, with a great deal of satisfaction.

"They'll be skatin' in hell a long time before they ever hang me," swore Angel.

"Oh, shut up," said Langley wearily. "No use snappin' at each other. We're all in on this deal. Let's plan what to do. How about makin' a break, boys? We might be lucky, eh?"

"Go ahead," said a voice outside the kitchen door. "We been wonderin' why yuh didn't."

"That's Hashknife Hartley's voice," said Fohl.

Angel swore hollowly. It sounded as though he was losing his nerve.

"How about the upstairs winders?" queried One-Eye. "We could drop to the ground, Jim."

"And get shot en route, eh?" sneered Fohl. "They'd be lookin' for us to do that."

Suddenly the front door banged open. Langley, who was on the floor in the connecting doorway, fired three times toward the doorway and then rolled into the corner. But there was no answering shot. Langley swore impotently. He had forgotten to lock the door.

"Keep out of line with the door," warned Langley.

"They're afraid of hurtin' the girl!" exclaimed Fohl. "By God, we've got the best of 'em, Jim!"

"Water," begged Briggs. "They're burnin' the house."

"Please get him some water," said Lila. "Won't somebody get him some water?"

"Don't pay any attention to him," said Angel.

Fohl swore angrily and began moving along the floor.

235

"I'll get yuh some water, Roper," he said. "I may want some myself pretty soon."

"Keep out of line with that door," warned Langley.

They heard Fohl rattling a dipper in the bucket, and in a moment he was slithering back along the floor. They could hear Briggs drinking the water.

"Thank you, Mr. Fohl," said Lila.

"Shut up!" growled Angel disgustedly.

"Don't thank me, miss," said Fohl. "Roper's my bunkie."

"What's the matter with everybody?" whispered Briggs. "It's so damned dark in here."

"Angel shot yuh, Roper. Don't yuh remember it?"

"He did? Where is he, Jess? He ain't here in the dark, is he? Oh, I remember now — that girl."

"Choke that fool off, will yuh?" rasped Angel.

"That's him!" panted Briggs. "I know his voice. Jess, I can't — my God, I'm as weak as a rabbit. Funny, ain't it? He hit me in the chest, Jess. I'm awful hot inside."

"What are they doin' outside?" wondered Langley.

"Fixin' to git us," said One-Eye, his voice filled with discouragement. "Let's send the girl out, Jim. She's what they want, anyway."

"Like hell, you will!" exploded Angel. "She's our ace-in-the-hole, you fool. As long as she's in here, they don't dare shoot at us."

"What's that noise?" asked Langley.

They listened closely. From the rear of the building came a sharp bump, followed by a scraping sound. None of the men were able to explain it. Langley crawled back into the front room and went to the window on the right-hand side, but it was so dark he could not see anything.

He slid along the wall toward the front of the room. That open front door intrigued him. Once in the open he would have a fighting chance, he thought. The rest of them could take care of themselves. He reached the doorway, where he waited, straining his ears for any sound. Except for the slight rustle of the wind, all was quiet.

He stretched out flat, gun in hand, and began inching over the doorsill. His belt-buckle caught on the sill, and he twisted sideways to release it, when something crashed down on his head and he ceased crawling. But he still continued to move slowly ahead across the porch, drawn by the arms of a man who chuckled softly. It sounded much like the chuckle of Sleepy Stevens.

Roper Briggs had been talking brokenly, deliriously.

"Where's Langley?" demanded Angel in a hoarse whisper.

"Over by one of the front winders," replied One-Eye.

"I think he went upstairs," said Fohl. "I heard him."

"I thought I heard him up there," said Angel. "I wish them damned fools would start somethin'."

"Don't worry — they will," assured Fohl. "You kidnapped Slim Caldwell's girl, yuh remember — and he's out there. Why didn't yuh rob a bank or kill somebody, instead of what yuh done? Give yoreself a fightin' chance, Angel."

"Jim's comin' down," said One-Eye.

237

They heard him crawling from the stairway, the knees of his overalls rasping softly on the floor.

"See anybody, Jim?" asked Fohl.

"No," he whispered. "Where are yuh, Angel?"

"Over here," growled Angel. "What do yuh want, Jim?"

"I've got a scheme."

"Make up your mind to come out, folks."

It was Slim Caldwell's voice, speaking near the kitchen door.

"You go to hell!" snapped Angel. "We're not comin' out. And lemme tell yuh somethin' else, Caldwell; this girl ain't comin' out neither. You start anythin', and she'll suffer for it."

Slim made no reply to Angel's threat. Came the sound of some one changing his position on the floor, a gurgle, which might have been a curse — the sound of a blow.

"What in hell was that?" demanded Fohl. "Angel, did you hit that girl?"

"I — I'm all right," gasped Lila. "What —"

"Fohl!"

It was not Jim Langley's voice.

"Who in hell was that?" asked One-Eye quickly. "That ain't Jim's voice!"

"What do yuh want?"

Fohl's voice was high-pitched, nervous.

"The game is up, boys," said Hashknife Hartley. "Unless I'm mistaken, Jim Langley is plumb safe. Angel is out of the fight. One of yuh light the lamp."

"Well, I'll be a liar!" exclaimed One-Eye. "It's Hartley, Jess. Go easy. My God, we're —"

"I'll light it," said Fohl. "I'm through; so don't shoot."

He managed to find the lamp, and after breaking several matches he lighted the wick. Hashknife squatted on his heels against the kitchen door, his six-shooter leveled from his knee, a grin on his lips. Angel was stretched out on his face, while nearer the corner was Lila, bracing herself on one elbow, wide-eyed, a smudge of dirt across her cheek.

Roper Briggs was lying against the opposite wall, his head fallen forward on his chest, and near him was One-Eye Connell, blinking his remaining optic at everything. Fohl had backed away from the table, where he had placed his gun, and was holding his hands shoulder-high.

"All right, cowboy?" yelled Sleepy from the front door.

"All set!" yelled Hashknife, and in came Sleepy, Slim, and Chuck, their guns ready for anything that might happen.

"Yuh kinda busted up the nest, didn't yuh?" laughed Sleepy.

Slim went straight to Lila and helped her to her feet. She was beyond words as she clung to his arm.

"It's all right," he told her.

"It's all right," echoed Jess Fohl. "We was a lot of fools to try and help him out. I'm glad we didn't hurt anybody, 'cause that kinda lets us out. Angel shot Roper Briggs."

Hashknife looked curiously at Fohl.

"Lets you out, eh?" He turned to Sleepy. "Go upstairs and get the old man."

"Old man who?" asked Sleepy.

"Old Rance McCoy."

Sleepy lighted another lamp and went up the stairs. Angel groaned and sat up, blinking foolishly. His eyes were dull and he swung his head like a sick animal.

"You must "a" popped him a good one, Hashknife," said Slim.

"I shore did. That old ladder done the trick. It let me in that upstairs window, and I was at the bottom of the stairs when I heard somebody get slugged at the front door. And then I heard somebody ask for Langley. I knew he was the missin' link; so I played Langley long enough to whisper to Angel with my gun barrel."

Angel sat up. His head was clearing fast, and his eyes flashed to Lila, who was standing close to Slim. No one was paying any attention to Roper Briggs, who had lifted his head and was peering across the room at Angel. Briggs had a gun beneath the crook of his knee, and his groping fingers closed around it.

Sleepy was coming back down the stairs, making plenty of noise. He was half-carrying old Rance McCoy, who was barefooted, naked to the waist, and hardly able to take a step.

"The old boy's in bad shape," panted Sleepy. "Don't sabe what it's all about. Cussed hell out of me."

As they turned to look at the old man, blinking in the lamplight, Angel grasped the corner of the table and surged to his feet. At the same instant he saw Jess

Fohl's six-shooter on the table, and as quick as a flash he grabbed it with his right hand.

"Damn yuh!" he choked. "My turn, by God! If yuh move I'll —"

But Angel didn't finish his threat. Roper Briggs had shot from his twisted position on the floor, and Angel buckled at the knees, striking his shoulders against the table, and falling backwards in the center of the room.

Roper chuckled and slid forward. The jar of the shot seemed to shock old Rance to a semblance of himself. He peered at Lila through the haze of powder smoke.

"Lila, why are you here?" he asked hoarsely. "What's it all about, anyway?"

"Angel kidnapped her, Rance," said Slim. "He was drunk and crazy. Langley is a prisoner, and I think Angel is dead."

"He's dead?" Old Rance limped forward, looking down at him.

Hashknife made a quick examination, nodding slowly.

"I'm sorry, Rance," he said. "He can't blame anybody."

"Let me set down," said Rance wearily. "Yuh see, they burned my feet tryin' to make me tell where the money was. But I didn't tell."

"Did Angel do that to yuh, Rance?"

"Not Angel — Langley. Angel wasn't in on it."

"The hell he wasn't!" snorted Fohl. "He was the one that framed it all, Rance."

"Yore own son," said Hashknife.

Rance looked curiously at Hashknife.

"He — he framed it all? He thought *I* robbed that train? My God, I thought he done it."

"You thought he knocked you down and robbed you the night of the robbery, didn't yuh, Rance?" asked Hashknife.

"I was pretty sure he did, and I didn't want anybody to suspect him, so I let 'em think I done it."

"Billy DuMond robbed you that night," said Hashknife. "But why did you take Angel's I.O.U. for seventy-eight hundred, Rance?"

"I never thought about DuMond doin' it. I — I wanted to help Angel out. He was busted, so I took his I.O.U."

"That's what Langley and Angel were tryin' to find at the Circle Spade," said Hashknife. "I thought it was."

"But did you know Rance was here?" asked Sleepy.

"Suspected it, Sleepy."

"Roper said yuh did," said Fohl. "He was scared."

"But Reimer and Kid Glover are in jail, Jess," said Chuck. "They've confessed to robbin' the train. Glover killed DuMond and Corby."

"My God!" blurted Fohl. "Old Rance didn't know anythin' about it — and Langley burned his feet to make him tell."

"It hurt like hell," said old Rance simply. He was staring at Angel, whose white face showed in the lamplight.

"Heredity," he said slowly. Then he looked up at Hashknife. "Do you believe in it, Hartley?"

"Not much."

Lila was looking at old Rance, her eyes wide.

"I didn't, Hartley. Jim Stevens did. He was educated, dyin' from consumption, but one of the whitest men God ever made. His wife went insane. Tried to kill him. They took her to the asylum, where she died."

Old Rance sighed heavily and shook his head wearily.

"I've kept still all these years, boys, but I'm tellin' it now. I was broke. My wife was dead and I had a kid to take care of, so I robbed a bank. But they blocked me, and I had to drop the money.

"I got away and headed for my shack. I knew I was caught, but I aimed to put up a fight. As I went through the doorway, I thought they had beat me to it. A man was there, and I shot him."

Old Rance looked around at the tense faces of the men.

"Yeah, I shot him. It was Jim Stevens — he came to see me. Poor old Jim — my only friend at that time. I told him what had happened and he forgave me. He said it didn't make any difference. I reckon I was half-crazy. And then he asked me if they had recognized me.

"I didn't think they had. And then he made me a proposition. Boys, it was a sneakin' thing to do; but I put my coat and hat on him, strapped my belt on him, took my extra gun and fired it down through a hole in the floor; so it wouldn't make much noise.

"Them men was comin'. They was sure the robber went to my cabin. But before they surrounded us, I went to the door and waved to 'em to come on. They found old Jim on the floor. I swore I didn't know what it was all about; that Jim ran in on me, and we swapped shots.

"They told me what Jim had done. They knowed he was the right man, because of that old gray coat. They took him away, wonderin' what would happen to Jim's kid; but I told 'em I'd take it. They knew old Jim was my friend, and none of 'em wanted the kid, anyway.

"But old Jim had my promise before he died. I swore I'd never let the kid know anythin' of the truth. Jim believed in heredity. He said it was partly a state of mind, and if the kid never knew — mebby it would be all right. And I never told anybody, boys. I kept my oath to old Jim Stevens. Even when things went ag'in' me — I stuck it out."

Lila went to him and put an arm around his shoulders.

"And they said you had no conscience," she sobbed. "Oh, I'm so sorry, Daddy Rance. I went away when you needed me, but I'm going to stay with you now. I don't believe in heredity."

Old Rance looked up at her, his eyes wet with tears.

"I'm a damned old fool, Lila," he said. "I sacrificed my own to keep my word. Don't you see what I mean, Lila? Jim Stevens's baby was a boy!"

For several moments no one said a word. They were trying to understand what old Rance meant.

"You — you mean — Angel?" whispered Lila.

Old Rance nodded quickly.

"Billy DuMond got it kinda twisted," he said. "I hope we can find some slippers around here; I can't wear boots."

"And you can all thank Hashknife," said Slim, looking around. "He dug it all out for us. Where's Hashknife?"

"Where's Sleepy?" asked Chuck.

But nobody knew. They had tiptoed their way out, mounted their horses, and were heading for Red Arrow, leaving the sheriff and Chuck to mop up things. Neither of them could stand to be thanked.

They found Scotty McKay at the office, along with a dozen other men, including Jim Parker. They were waiting some word from Slim regarding Lila, and almost mobbed Hashknife and Sleepy for information.

"She's safe," said Hashknife. "Angel McCoy and Roper Briggs are dead; they shot each other. Angel kidnapped Lila to get back at Slim, and upset the lamp in Parker's house. Rance McCoy is all right. Langley and his gang were tryin' to force him to tell where the loot from the express car was cached. Slim is bringin' 'em all in, and you'll get the whole story from him. Was there any telegram, Scotty?"

Wonderingly Scotty handed Hashknife the telegram, which had been sent to Slim Caldwell. It read:

PAULSEN CONFESSED ARREST REIMER GLOVER DUMOND CONGRATULATIONS YOU WIN THE REWARD

WELLS FARGO

Hashknife grinned and handed the telegram back to Scotty.

"Well, that shore settles it," he said. "C'mon, Sleepy."

CHAPTER
TWENTY-TWO

The Trail Again

The crowd stepped aside and let them go. No one said anything. Possibly the men were so shocked over what had happened that night that they didn't know what to say.

Hashknife and Sleepy went to the hotel and got their war-bags, mounted their horses, and rode southward out of Red Arrow. Someone called to them from the sheriff's office, but they did not heed. Their work was over, and nothing remained to be done.

"It shore feels good to have a *horse* between yore legs again, Sleepy," said Hashknife. "That Half-Box R bay was all right, but nothin' like Ghost. It's funny what a simple horse trade will lead to. Kid Glover's bay picks up a sharp rock, and from there she rolls bigger and bigger, like a snowball rollin' down a hill. But it was all right, pardner. We'll get to Arizona before snow flies in this country. Things like this kinda break the monotony, don'tcha know it?"

"There was five thousand dollars reward," reminded Sleepy.

"Yeah, there was. And it'll be a good thing for Slim and Lila to start housekeepin' on."

246

"Yeah, that's true, Hashknife. It was plenty fun, but not a bit remunerative."

"It ain't what yuh get, Sleepy; it's what yuh learn."

"What in hell didja learn?"

"I learned that when an old jigger like Rance McCoy gives his word, it makes blood a sight thinner than water."

"Shore; but what good will that ever do you?"

"It builds up my faith in humanity."

"Anyway, we got yore horse, Hashknife; and that's what we went after."

"Which is all anybody could ask, pardner."

And they rode on toward Arizona — satisfied — while back in Red Arrow the people wondered where they had gone. Butch Reimer returned the money, and the judge gave him few enough years for his crime. Kid Glover paid the penalty of his murders, while Langley, Fohl, and One-Eye Connell served short terms.

Rance McCoy got his money back which DuMond stole that night, and later he sold the Eagle for enough to pay him back the money he had lost on a crooked deal. Slim Caldwell resigned his office when he married Lila McCoy, and went into business with the Circle Spade, where Chuckwalla still putters around the kitchen, testing out new recipes from a cook book, which had been sent him from Arizona.

There was no mark on it to show who sent it, except on the cover, where a crudely drawn hashknife gave them a clue to the donor. Lila tore off the cover and had it framed; and it hangs over the fireplace of the Circle Spade ranchhouse.

247

Chuck Ring is sheriff now, wishing for something to happen again. And somewhere under the sun, heading toward the next hill, ride Hashknife and Sleepy, looking into the future with a smile — following the dim trails.

ISIS publish a wide range of books in large print, from fiction to biography. Any suggestions for books you would like to see in large print or audio are always welcome. Please send to the Editorial Department at:

ISIS Publishing Limited
7 Centremead
Osney Mead
Oxford OX2 0ES

A full list of titles is available free of charge from:

Ulverscroft Large Print Books Limited

(UK)
The Green
Bradgate Road, Anstey
Leicester LE7 7FU
Tel: (0116) 236 4325

(Australia)
P.O. Box 314
St Leonards
NSW 1590
Tel: (02) 9436 2622

(USA)
P.O. Box 1230
West Seneca
N.Y. 14224-1230
Tel: (716) 674 4270

(Canada)
P.O. Box 80038
Burlington
Ontario L7L 6B1
Tel: (905) 637 8734

(New Zealand)
P.O. Box 456
Feilding
Tel: (06) 323 6828

Details of **ISIS** complete and unabridged audio books are also available from these offices. Alternatively, contact your local library for details of their collection of **ISIS** large print and unabridged audio books.